PENGUIN CLASSICS
Maigret in Vichy

'I love reading Simenon.

— William Faulkner

'A truly wonderful writer . . . marvellously readable – lucid, simple, absolutely in tune with the world he creates'

— Muriel Spark

'Few writers have ever conveyed with such a sure touch, the bleakness of human life' — A. N. Wilson

'One of the greatest writers of the twentieth century . . . Simenon was unequalled at making us look inside, though the ability was masked by his brilliance at absorbing us obsessively in his stories' — *Guardian*

'A novelist who entered his fictional world as if he were part of it' — Peter Ackroyd

'The greatest of all, the most genuine novelist we have had in literature' — André Gide

'Superb . . . The most addictive of writers . . . A unique teller of tales' — *Observer*

'The mysteries of the human personality are revealed in all their disconcerting complexity' — Anita Brookner

'A writer who, more than any other crime novelist, combined a high literary reputation with popular appeal'

— P. D. James

'A supreme writer . . . Unforgettable vividness'

— *Independent*

'Compelling, remorseless, brilliant' — John Gray

'Extraordinary masterpieces of the twentieth century'

— John Banville

GEORGES SIMENON

Maigret in Vichy

Translated by ROS SCHWARTZ

PENGUIN BOOKS

PENGUIN CLASSICS

UK | USA | Canada | Ireland | Australia
India | New Zealand | South Africa

Penguin Books is part of the Penguin Random House group of companies
whose addresses can be found at global.penguinrandomhouse.com.

First published in serial, as *Maigret à Vichy*, in *Le Figaro* 1968
First published in book form by Presses de la Cité 1968
This translation first published 2019
001

Set in 12.5/15 pt Dante MT Std
Typeset by Jouve (UK), Milton Keynes
Printed and bound in Great Britain by Clays Ltd, Elcograf S.p.A.

ISBN: 978-0-241-30421-1

www.greenpenguin.co.uk

Penguin Random House is committed to a
sustainable future for our business, our readers
and our planet. This book is made from Forest
Stewardship Council® certified paper.

Maigret in Vichy

1.

'Do you know them?' Madame Maigret asked in an under-tone as her husband turned around to look at a couple they had just passed.

The man had also turned around and was smiling. He even gave the impression he was about to retrace his steps to shake Maigret's hand.

'No . . . I don't think so . . . I don't know . . .'

The man was short and stout, his wife barely taller than him and podgy. Why did Maigret have the feeling that she was Belgian? Because of her fair complexion, her almost yellow hair and her bulging blue eyes?

This was the fifth time at least that their paths had crossed. The first time, the man had stopped dead and his face had lit up as if in delight. Hesitant, he had half-opened his mouth, while Maigret frowned and racked his brains in vain.

The man's physique and face looked familiar. But who the devil could he be? Where had he met this cheerful little fellow and his marzipan wife before?

'Honestly, I can't think . . .'

It wasn't important. Besides, the people here were not the same as in normal life. Any moment now, the music would strike up. On the bandstand, with its spindly columns and ornate decorations, the uniformed musicians were raising their brass instruments to their lips, their eyes on the conductor. Was it the firemen's band or the municipal workers? They had as many decorations and stripes as South American generals, blood-red shoulder straps and white baldrics.

Hundreds of yellow iron chairs were arranged around the bandstand, in ever-widening circles as far as the eye could see, and nearly all of them were occupied by men and women waiting in solemn silence.

In a couple of minutes' time, at nine o'clock, under the spreading trees in the park, the concert would begin. After a muggy day, the evening air was almost chilly, and the breeze made the leaves rustle softly while the light from the rows of lamp posts with milky globes made pools of a paler green on the dark grass.

'Don't you want to sit down?'

There were a few free chairs, but they never sat down. They walked at a leisurely pace. Other visitors were strolling around aimlessly like them, half listening to the music, couples, but also many on their own, men and women who were nearly all past middle age.

It was a little unreal. The casino was lit up, white and sumptuous with over-elaborate 1900s-style mouldings. At certain moments, time seemed to have stood still, until a car horn sounded on Rue Georges-Clemenceau.

'She's here . . .' whispered Madame Maigret, jerking her chin.

It had turned into a game. She'd got into the habit of following her husband's gaze and she could tell when he was surprised or intrigued.

What else did they have to do with their days? They ambled around casually. From time to time, they paused, not because they were out of breath but to admire a tree, a house, the play of light and shadow, or a face.

They could have sworn they'd been in Vichy for an eternity, whereas this was only their fifth day. They had already created a schedule for themselves which they followed meticulously as if it were of the utmost importance, and their days were measured out by various rituals which they adhered to religiously.

Was Maigret really being serious? His wife sometimes wondered, darting furtive glances at him. He was different from when they were in Paris. His step was more languid, his expression less intense. Most of the time, his vague smile expressed satisfaction, certainly, but also a sort of gloomy irony.

'She's wearing her white stole . . .'

From roaming the park and the banks of the Allier, the boulevards lined with plane trees and the teeming or deserted streets at the same time every day, they had come to recognize a number of faces and figures that were already part of their world.

Did not everyone here replicate the same actions at the same time of day, and not only at the springs where they drank their hallowed beakers of water?

Maigret's gaze picked out someone in the crowd and became more focused. That of his wife followed.

'Do you think she's a widow?'

They could have nicknamed her the lady in mauve, or rather the lady in lilac, because she always wore something lilac-coloured. That evening, she must have arrived late and had only managed to find at seat at the back.

The previous day, she had afforded a sight that was both unexpected and moving. The Maigrets had walked past the bandstand at eight o'clock in the evening, one hour before the concert. The little yellow chairs were arranged in circles so regular that they could have been drawn with a compass.

All the chairs were empty, except one in the front row, where the lady in lilac was sitting. She was not reading by the light of the nearest lamp. She was not knitting. She was doing nothing, showing no impatience. Sitting upright, with both hands resting flat on her knees, she remained absolutely still, staring straight ahead, cutting a distinguished figure.

She looked as if she had come straight out of a picture book. She wore a white hat, whereas most of the women here were bareheaded. The stole around her shoulders was white too, and her dress the lilac colour of which she seemed fond.

Her face was very long and narrow, her lips thin.

'She must be a spinster, don't you think?'

Maigret avoided saying anything. He wasn't on a case, wasn't following any leads. Nothing was forcing him to watch people to try and discover their inner truth.

He couldn't help doing so, now and then, because it had become a reflex. For no reason, he sometimes took an interest in a person out for a stroll, and tried to guess their profession, their family circumstances and the kind of life they led when they weren't taking the waters.

It was difficult. After a few days or a few hours, everyone became part of the little circle . . . Most eyes had the same slightly vacant serenity, apart from those of the very sick, who were recognizable by their deformities, their gait, but especially from a mixture of anxiety and hope.

The lady in lilac was among those who could have been called Maigret's inner circle, the people he'd noticed from the start and who intrigued him.

It was hard to fathom her age. She could just as easily have been forty-five or fifty-five and the years had passed her by without leaving any particular scars.

One could guess she was used to living in silence, as with nuns, accustomed to solitude. Perhaps she even preferred that solitude. Whether walking or sitting, as she was at present, she paid no attention to promenaders or to her neighbours, and she would probably have been most surprised to learn that outside of any professional obligation, Detective Chief Inspector Maigret was trying to gauge her personality.

'I don't think she's ever lived with a man . . .' he said as the music struck up on the bandstand.

'Or with children. Perhaps with a very elderly person needing care, an aged mother, for example?'

In that case, she couldn't be a very good nurse because she lacked gentleness and the gift of communication. If her gaze did not light on people but slid over them without seeing them, it was because it was turned inwards. It was herself, and only herself, that she looked at, and she probably derived a secret satisfaction from doing so.

'Shall we walk around the park?'

They weren't there to listen to the music. It was simply part of their routine to go past the bandstand at that time, and besides, there wasn't a concert every day.

On some evenings, that area of the park was almost deserted. They strolled across it, turned right, and set out down the tree-lined avenue that ran parallel to a street full of neon signs. There were hotels, restaurants, shops and a cinema. They hadn't been there yet, it wasn't on their itinerary.

Some people were following the same route, almost at the same pace, others were going in the opposite direction. A few took a shortcut to the casino theatre where they'd arrive late, and there were glimpses of the occasional dinner-jacket or evening gown.

Elsewhere, these folk led different lives, in different neighbourhoods of Paris, in provincial towns or in Brussels, Amsterdam, Rome or Philadelphia.

They belonged to particular social circles that had their rules, their taboos and their passwords. Some were wealthy, others poor. There were invalids whose lives the treatment merely prolonged, and others whom it enabled to spend the rest of the year without having to worry too much about their health.

Here, they all mingled. For Maigret, it had all begun uneventfully, one evening when they were having dinner at the Pardons'. Madame Pardon had cooked pressed duck, one of her specialities, which Maigret loved.

'Isn't it any good?' she'd asked anxiously, seeing Maigret eat only a few mouthfuls.

Whereas Pardon suddenly looked at his guest with concern.

'Are you in pain?'

'Not really . . . It's nothing . . .'

Even so, the doctor noticed that his friend's face was pale and that there were beads of sweat on his forehead.

He said no more during the meal. Maigret had barely taken a sip from his glass. When offered a vintage Armagnac with the coffee, he raised his hand.

'Not tonight . . . I'm sorry . . .'

Only later, Pardon said quietly:

'Shall we go into my consulting room for a moment?'

Maigret followed him reluctantly. For some time he had foreseen that this would happen one day, but he kept postponing that day. The doctor's consulting room was neither big nor luxurious. On the desk a stethoscope lay next to vials, tubes of ointment and paperwork, and the bed where patients were examined seemed to have retained the deep imprint of the last one.

'What's wrong, Maigret?'

'I don't know. Age, probably . . .'

'Fifty-two?'

'Fifty-three . . . I've had a lot of work recently, worries . . . No sensational cases . . . Nothing exciting, on the contrary . . . On the one hand, lots of red tape, because we're in the middle of overhauling the Police Judiciaire, and on the other, this spate of attacks on lone girls and women, sometimes involving rape . . . The press is making a hoo-ha and I don't have enough men to set up the necessary patrols without decimating the department . . .'

'Are you having problems with your digestion?'

'Occasionally . . . Sometimes, like this evening, my

stomach's in a knot, I have pain, or rather a sort of tightening of my chest and abdomen . . . I feel heavy, tired . . .'

'Would you mind if I examined you?'

His wife, in the next room, must have guessed, Madame Pardon too, and that bothered Maigret. He had a horror of anything even remotely connected with illness.

As he removed his tie, jacket, shirt and vest, he recalled one of his adolescent notions.

'I can't live,' he'd announced at the time, 'with pills, potions, a diet, reduced activity. I'd rather die than be an invalid . . .'

His idea of 'an invalid' was someone who was forever listening to their heart, worrying about their stomach, their liver or their kidneys, and exhibiting their naked body to the doctor on a regular basis.

He no longer wished to die young, but he was putting off the time when he would become ill.

'My trousers too?'

'Drop them a little . . .'

Pardon took his blood pressure, examined him and felt his stomach and abdomen, pressing certain places with his fingers.

'Does that hurt?'

'No . . . Maybe a little tender . . . No, lower . . .'

Now he was like the others, anxious, ashamed of his fears and not daring to look his friend in the face. He got dressed again, awkwardly. Pardon's tone hadn't changed.

'How long is it since you've had a holiday?'

'Last year I managed to get away for a week, then I was called back because—'

'What about the previous year?'

'I stayed in Paris . . .'

'With the life you lead, your organs should be in five times worse shape than they are—'

'My liver?'

'It has nobly withstood the strain you put it under . . . It's slightly enlarged, for certain, but not hugely swollen, and it has maintained its elasticity . . .'

'What's wrong?'

'Nothing specific . . . More or less everything . . . You're tired, that's a fact, and it's not a one-week holiday that will rid you of that fatigue . . . How do you feel when you wake up in the morning?'

'Crabby . . .'

That made Pardon laugh.

'Do you sleep well?'

'My wife says I'm restless and that I sometimes talk in my sleep . . .'

'You're not filling your pipe?'

'I'm trying to smoke less.'

'Why?'

'I don't know . . . I'm also trying to drink less . . .'

'Have a seat.'

Pardon sat down too, and, at his desk, looked more like a doctor than in the dining room or the living room.

'Now listen to me . . . You're not ill and you enjoy exceptional good health given your age and your occupation . . . So get that into your head once and for all . . . Stop worrying about the odd twinge and vague aches and pains, and don't start being nervous about climbing stairs—'

'How do you know?'

'And you, when you question a suspect, how do you know?'

They both smiled.

'Now we're in late June. Paris is sweltering. You are going to take a nice holiday, without leaving an address, if possible. In any case, you must avoid telephoning Quai des Orfèvres every day . . .'

'I could do,' said Maigret gruffly. 'Our little house in Meung-sur-Loire—'

'You'll have time to enjoy that once you've retired . . . This year, I have other plans for you. Do you know Vichy?'

'I've never set foot there, even though I was born less than fifty kilometres away, near Moulins . . . In those days, people didn't all have cars . . .'

'By the way, does your wife have a driving licence?'

'We've even bought a four-CV . . .'

'I think that a course of treatment at Vichy would do you the world of good . . . A thorough cleansing of your body . . .'

He nearly burst out laughing on seeing Maigret's expression.

'Take the waters?'

'A few glasses of water each day . . . I don't think the specialist will make you sit in mud baths or hot springs, or prescribe mechanotherapy and all that nonsense . . . You're not a serious case . . . Twenty-one days of a regular lifestyle, without any worries—'

'Without beer, without wine, without eating out, without—'

'How many years have you been indulging?'

'I've had my share . . .' he admitted.

'And you'll have more, even if that share is slightly reduced . . . Is that agreed?'

Maigret was amazed to hear himself say, as he stood up, like any other of Pardon's patients:

'It's agreed.'

'When?'

'In a few days' time, a week at most, once I've tied up all the loose ends . . .'

'I'm going to refer you to one of my colleagues there who's more knowledgeable about these things than I am . . . I know half a dozen specialists . . . Let's see . . . Rian is still young and isn't at all pompous . . . I'll give you his address and telephone number . . . I'll write to him tomorrow to inform him.'

'Thank you, Pardon . . .'

'That wasn't too painful, was it?'

'You were very gentle.'

In the living room, he gave his wife a reassuring smile, but they didn't talk about illness at the Pardons.

It was only when they reached Rue Popincourt, walking arm in arm, that Maigret muttered, as if it was something unimportant:

'We're spending our holiday in Vichy . . .'

'Are you going to take the waters?'

'May as well, while I'm there!' He laughed. 'I'm not ill. Apparently, I'm in exceptionally good health. That's why I'm being sent to drink water . . .'

It didn't just date from that visit to Pardon. For some time he'd had the strange impression that everyone was younger than him, whether it was the prefect or the examining magistrates, defendants he was questioning or, now, this Doctor Rian, who was fair-haired and affable and not yet forty.

A kid, in other words, a young man at the most, nevertheless earnest and self-assured, who was going to decide his fate.

This thought both annoyed and worried him, because he didn't feel like an old man, or even one who was ageing.

Despite his youthfulness, Doctor Rian lived in a pretty pink-brick residence on Boulevard des États-Unis and, while the décor was reminiscent of the 1900s, it was still opulent-looking, with its marble staircases, carpets, polished furniture and the maid in a frilly broderie-anglaise cap.

'I presume your parents are no longer living . . . ? What did your father die of?'

The doctor wrote his replies down on an index card, painstakingly, in the calligraphic style characteristic of a Sergeant-Major nib pen.

'What about your mother . . . ? Do you have any brothers . . . ? Sisters . . . ? Childhood illnesses . . . ? Measles . . . ? Scarlet fever . . . ?'

Not scarlet fever but measles, very young, when his mother had still been alive. It was even the warmest, most comforting memory he had of her, because he was to lose her shortly afterwards.

'What sports have you played . . . ? No accidents . . . ? Do you often get throat infections . . . ? Heavy smoker, I presume . . . ?'

The young doctor smiled mischievously, to show Maigret that he knew him by reputation.

'One could say that you have led a sedentary life . . .'

'It all depends. Sometimes I spend three weeks or a month in my office all day long and then suddenly I'm out and about for several days . . .'

'Regular meals?'

'No . . .'

'You don't follow a diet of any kind?'

Was he not obliged to admit that he loved slow-cooked dishes, stews and sauces of every imaginable flavour?

'Not just a food lover, but a big eater, eh?'

'Quite big, yes . . .'

'What about wine? Half a litre? A litre a day?'

'Yes . . . No . . . More . . . With meals, I usually have just two or three glasses . . . At the office, sometimes a beer, which I have sent up from a nearby brasserie.'

'Aperitif?'

'Quite often, with one or another of my colleagues . . .'

At the Brasserie Dauphine. It wasn't to get drunk but for the atmosphere, the familiar crush, the smell of cooking, aniseed and calvados that had impregnated the walls. Why was he ashamed of it all of a sudden, in front of this young man who was so spruce and so comfortably housed?

'In short, no real excesses . . .'

He wanted to be honest.

'It depends what you call excesses. In the evenings, I don't say no to a glass or two of sloe brandy which my sister-in-law sends us from Alsace . . . My investigations often require me to spend a certain amount of time in cafés or bars . . . It's hard to explain . . . If I start one of these investigations on Vouvray, for example, because I find myself in a bar specializing in it, I tend to continue on Vouvray.'

'How many a day?'

This reminded him of his childhood, the village confessional redolent of mouldy old wood and the priest who snorted snuff.

'A lot?'

'You'd probably say it was a lot . . .'

'Does it go on for long?'

'Sometimes three days, sometimes eight or ten if not more. It depends on luck . . .'

The doctor didn't reprimand him. He wasn't given a rosary to recite, but he could guess what the fair-haired doctor, sitting in the sunlight, behind a fine mahogany desk, thought of him.

'No severe indigestion? No heartburn, dizziness . . . ?'

Dizziness, yes. Nothing serious. Occasionally, especially over the past few weeks, he felt as if he were in a less solid world that was slightly unreal. He himself was floating, his legs wobbly.

It wasn't bad enough to seriously worry him, but it was unpleasant. Luckily this sensation only lasted a few minutes. Once, it had happened when he was about to cross Boulevard du Palais and he'd waited before venturing into the road.

'I see . . . I see . . .'

What did he see? That he was ill? That he smoked and drank too much? That it was time, at his age, to go on a diet?

Maigret wasn't dismayed. He smiled, with the smile his

wife had seen on his face since they'd been in Vichy. He appeared to be laughing at himself, but even so he was a little dispirited.

'Let us go next door . . .'

The whole works this time! The doctor even made him climb up and down the rungs of a stepladder for three minutes. Blood pressure lying down, sitting and standing. Then the screen.

'Breathe . . . Deeper . . . Hold your breath . . . Breathe in . . . Hold it . . . Breathe out . . .'

It was funny and upsetting, dramatic and crazy. He had another thirty years to live, perhaps, but it was equally possible that in a few minutes he'd be told tactfully that his life as a man in good health, as a normal man, was over and that from now on he would be an invalid.

They had all been through the same thing, all the people they met in the park, around the springs, under the luxuriant trees, by the lake, and even those who sunbathed on the beach, the boules players, the tennis players glimpsed on the other side of the Allier in the shade of the Sporting Club.

'Mademoiselle Jeanne . . .'

'Yes, monsieur . . .'

The nurse knew what she had to bring. It was all part of a routine like the one the Maigrets were going to adopt.

First of all, the little device to prick his fingertip and collect drops of blood that would be divided among several test tubes.

'Relax . . . Clench your fist . . .'

A needle pricked the vein in his arm.

'Unclench . . .'

This wasn't the first time he'd had his blood taken, but it felt as if this time the test had taken on a sort of solemnity.

'Thank you . . . You can put your clothes back on now.'

They met up again in the office whose walls were lined with books and medical journals bound year by year.

'I don't think heavy medication is required in your case . . . I'll see you the day after tomorrow at the same time, when I'll have the results of your tests . . . In the meantime, I've devised a regimen for you . . . You're staying at a hotel, I assume . . . ? Just give this sheet to the hotel manager . . . He'll know what to do.'

A printed card with two columns: in one, dishes that were allowed, and in the other, dishes that were prohibited. There were even sample menus on the back.

'I don't know whether you're aware of the therapeutic benefits of the various springs. There used to be a little book on the subject, written by two of my colleagues, but I think it's out of print . . . We're going to try, first of all, to alternate the waters of two springs, Chomel and Grande Grille, both of which you'll find in the park . . .'

The two men were solemn. Maigret didn't feel like shrugging or laughing while the doctor scribbled on a notepad.

'Are you in the habit of rising early and having breakfast . . . ? I see . . . Is your wife here with you . . . ? In that case, I shan't send you across town on an empty stomach . . . Let's see . . . Start in the morning, at around ten thirty, at the Grande Grille . . . You'll find chairs to sit on and, if it's raining, a big glazed hall . . . Drink a glass of water every half-hour, three times, as hot as you can manage . . .

'In the afternoon, at around five, do the same thing at the Chomel spring . . .

'Don't be surprised if, the next day, you feel a bit lethargic . . . It's a temporary effect of the treatment . . . Besides, I'll see you again then . . .'

All that was already ages ago. Then he was just a novice confusing one spring with another. Now, he was settled into the treatment routine, like the thousands, the tens of thousands of men and women he rubbed shoulders with from morning to evening.

Sometimes all the little yellow chairs in the park were taken, like in the evening, around the bandstand, each person waiting until it was time to go and drink their second, third or fourth dose.

Like the others, he'd bought a measuring glass and Madame Maigret had insisted on having her own.

'But you're not taking the waters.'

'Why not? What harm can it do? I read in the brochures that the waters make you lose weight . . .'

The glasses were kept in woven-straw cases and Madame Maigret wore both of them over her shoulder the way racegoers wear their binoculars.

The two of them had never been for so many walks. They were outdoors from nine o'clock in the morning and, apart from delivery men, they were almost the only people in the quiet streets of the neighbourhood they were staying in, the France district, close to the Célestins spring.

A few minutes from their hotel there was a children's playground, with a paddling pool, swings, games of all kinds and even a puppet theatre that was bigger than the one on the Champs-Élysées.

'Do you have your ticket, monsieur?'

They had paid one franc each and strolled beneath the trees, watching the almost naked kids frolicking, and had come back the next day.

'If you buy a book of twenty tickets, it'll be cheaper . . .'

He didn't dare. It was too premeditated. They had walked past by chance. It was only out of habit, out of idleness that they came back each day at the same time.

After that, they also stopped at the area reserved for the boules players, and Maigret solemnly watched two or three games, seeing under the same tree the tall, thin man who only had one arm but was the best thrower.

In another foursome, where the accent of the South could be heard, an elegantly dressed man with a rosy complexion and very white hair played with dignity, and the others called him 'senator'.

A little further on, the beach began, with the coastguards' hut and the buoys marking out the bathing area, and there too sat the same people under the same beach umbrellas.

'Aren't you bored?' his wife had asked him on the second day.

'Why?' he asked in surprise.

Because he wasn't bored. He was gradually adapting to a new pace, different habits. He noticed with amazement that he automatically filled his pipe on arriving at the Bellerive Bridge. And he filled another at the Yacht Club where, from the shore, they watched the young boys and girls water-skiing.

'Don't you think it's a dangerous sport?'

'Why?'

And finally the park, the glasses of water which a member of staff filled for them from the spring and which they sipped slowly. The water was hot and salty. At the Chomel spring, the water tasted strongly of sulphur, and Maigret hastily lit a fresh pipe.

Madame Maigret was astounded to find him so docile, so calm, and sometimes it even worried her.

That was when she found out that in a way he was playing the detective. He studied people, as if he couldn't help it, noted the slightest details and classified them by category. For example, at their hotel, the Hôtel de la Bérézina, a sort of family guesthouse, he had already identified from their diet those with liver problems and the diabetics.

He tried to guess each person's story, to imagine them in their everyday life and, sometimes, he got his wife to join in this pastime.

He was fascinated by the two he nicknamed 'the merry couple', the plump man who always looked as if he was about to come over and shake his hand, and his little wife who resembled a piece of candy. What could their occupation be? Had they recognized Maigret from seeing his photo in the newspapers?

In actual fact, not many people here recognized him, a lot fewer than in Paris. Admittedly his wife had made him buy a light, almost white, mohair jacket, like the ones worn by men of a certain age in the summer when he was a child.

Even without the jacket, people would probably not have

thought it was him. He was certain that those who frowned on glancing at him, or who turned around, said to themselves: 'Fancy that! He looks just like Maigret . . .'

But they didn't think he was Maigret. And, in truth, he was so little like himself!

The other intriguing character . . . The lady in lilac . . . She was taking the waters too, only at the Grande Grille, where they saw her every morning. She had her spot, slightly apart from everyone else, close to the newspaper kiosk. Always dignified and aloof, she only took one sip of water at a time, then, after rinsing and wiping her glass, she carefully put it back in its straw case.

Three or four people greeted her. The Maigrets didn't see her in the afternoons. Did she go to the baths? Had her doctor ordered her to rest?

'Sedimentation rate, perfect,' Doctor Rian had declared. 'Hourly average: 6 millimetres . . . Cholesterol a little high, but within the acceptable range . . . Urea normal . . . Serum iron level fairly low, but nothing to worry about . . . Nor about the uric acid . . . You're not allowed to eat game, offal or shellfish . . . As for your blood count, it is excellent, with a haemoglobin level of 98 . . .

'All you need is a thorough cleansing of your system . . . Do you not feel sluggish or get headaches . . . ? So we're going to continue with the same regimen for the next few days . . . Come and see me on Saturday.'

That evening, which was a bandstand concert evening, they didn't see the lady in lilac leave because they never stayed to the end of the concert but returned early to the France neighbourhood with its empty streets, freshly painted façades and the Hôtel de la Bérézina, whose double entrance door was flanked by two shrubs in containers.

They slept in a brass bed and all the furniture was from the turn of the century, like the clawfoot bathtub and the swan-neck taps.

The hotel was well run and quiet, except when the Gagnaires' son, who was on the first floor, played cowboys and Indians on his own in the garden.

Everyone was asleep.

Day five? Day six? It was Madame Maigret who was the most disoriented at not having to make coffee in the mornings. At seven o'clock, they were served breakfast on a tray, with fresh croissants and the Clermont-Ferrand newspaper, which devoted two pages to Vichy life.

Maigret had got into the habit of reading it from the first line to the last, so as to be informed of every single little local event. He even read the death notices and the classified ads.

'Three-bed house, bathroom, all mod cons, excellent condition, uninterrupted view over . . .'

'Do you intend to buy a house?'

'No, but it's interesting. I wonder whether it's people who regularly take the waters keen to have their own house to spend one month a year in, or whether it's retired folk from Paris or elsewhere who . . .'

They got dressed in turn and the owner never failed to greet them at the foot of the red-carpeted staircase with its brass rods. The owner wasn't from the area but from Mon-télimar, which could be detected from his singsong accent.

They frittered away the hours . . . The children's play-ground . . . The boules players . . .

'By the way, I saw that there's a big market every Wednesday and Saturday . . . We could go and have a look . . .'

He'd always loved markets, the smell of the fruit and vegetables, the sight of quarters of beef, fish, lobsters still alive . . .

'After all, Rian did tell me to walk five kilometres every day . . .'

His tone was ironic.

'He has no idea that we chalk up an average of fifteen!'

'Do you think?'

'Work it out . . . We walk for at least five hours . . . We might not walk at an athlete's pace, but we still do between three and four kilometres an hour . . .'

'I'd never have believed it . . .'

The glass of water. The yellow chair, and reading the Paris newspapers which had just arrived. Lunch in the all-white dining room where, on some tables, there was an opened bottle of wine labelled with the guest's name. There wasn't one on the Maigrets' table.

'Did he say you can't drink wine?'

'Not in so many words, but I may as well not . . .'

She couldn't get over seeing him become a conscientious spa patient and managing to remain good-humoured.

He allowed himself a brief nap, then they resumed their routine, on the other side of the town this time, with the parade of shops and the crowds on the pavements that kept forcing them apart.

'Have you noticed how many pedicurists and orthopaedists there are?'

'If everyone walks as much as we do . . . !'

There was no bandstand concert that evening, but there was one in the gardens of the Grand Casino. The brass band was replaced by string instruments and the music was more solemn, like the faces of the audience.

They didn't spot the lady in lilac, nor did they come across her walking in the park. But they did run into the merry couple, who were more dressed up than usual and hurrying in the direction of the casino theatre where a comedy was being performed.

The brass bed. Time flew by surprisingly fast, even though they were doing nothing. The croissants, coffee, the sugar lumps wrapped in waxed paper, the Clermont-Ferrand newspaper.

Maigret, in his armchair by the window, smoked his first pipe in his pyjamas, with some coffee still left in his cup, which he eked out as long as possible.

When he let out an exclamation, Madame Maigret appeared from the bathroom in a blue floral dressing gown, toothbrush in hand.

'What is it?'

'Look . . .'

On the first page devoted to Vichy was a photograph, that of the lady in lilac. She must have been a few years younger and she'd made the effort to give a wan smile for the photographer.

'What's happened to her?'

'She's been murdered . . .'

'Last night?'

'If it happened last night, it wouldn't be in today's papers . . . The night before . . .'

'We saw her at the bandstand . . .'

'At around nine o'clock, yes . . . She went home, two streets from here, Rue du Bourbonnais . . . I had no idea we were almost neighbours. She took off her stole and her hat, and went into the sitting room, on the left of the hallway—'

'How was she killed?'

'She was strangled . . . Yesterday morning, her lodgers were surprised not to hear any noise coming from the ground floor—'

'She's not here to take the waters?'

'She lives in Vichy all year round . . . She owns the house and rents out furnished rooms on the first floor.'

Maigret remained seated and his wife knew what an effort that was for him.

'Do you think it's a financially motivated murder?'

'The killer searched the place thoroughly, but doesn't appear to have taken anything . . . A few pieces of jewellery and a sum of money were even found in a drawer that had been opened . . .'

'She wasn't—'

'Raped? No . . .'

He gazed at the window in silence.

'Do you know who's in charge of the investigation?'

'Of course not.'

'Lecoeur, who was one of my inspectors and is now head of the Clermont-Ferrand Police Judiciaire . . . He's here . . . He doesn't have any idea that I am too . . .'

'Do you plan to go and see him?'

Maigret didn't answer straight away.

2.

It was five to nine and Maigret still hadn't answered his wife's question. It was as if it was a matter of honour for him to behave exactly as on the other mornings and keep to their Vichy routine without departing from it in the least.

He had read the newspaper to the end as he finished his coffee, then shaved, listening to the news on the radio as usual. At five to nine he was ready and the two of them descended the red-carpeted staircase with brass rods.

The owner, in a white jacket, a chef's hat on his head, was waiting for him in the hallway.

'Well, Monsieur Maigret, we're taking good care of you here in Vichy! Even going so far as to offer you a juicy murder . . .'

Maigret managed a vague smile.

'You'll be handling it, I hope?'

'What happens outside Paris isn't under my authority . . .'

Madame Maigret was watching him. She thought he wouldn't notice, but he was aware of it. Instead of going down Rue d'Auvergne, towards the river and the children's playground, he turned right, looking all innocent.

True, they sometimes varied their itinerary, but always on the way back from town. She was in awe of her husband's sense of direction. He hadn't consulted any maps. He gave the impression of wandering aimlessly, diving down little backstreets that seemed to be taking him away from his destination, and she'd be taken by surprise when she suddenly recognized the façade of their hotel, the two shrubs in their green containers.

This time he turned right again, then again, and they spotted a dozen or so onlookers on a pavement gazing upwards.

A little glint came into Madame Maigret's eyes. Maigret appeared to hesitate. He crossed to the other side of the street, stopped to empty his pipe, banging it against his heel, and slowly filled another. It made him look like a big child, and at times like these she felt a rush of affection.

A struggle was taking place inside Maigret. Finally, as if he didn't know where he was, he mingled with the group of curious spectators, and he too stared up at the house opposite, outside which a car was parked, and nearby a police officer was standing guard.

The house was elegant, like most of the others in the street. The façade had been repainted white tinged with pink quite recently, and the shutters and balcony were almond green.

On a marble plaque was the name, in fancy English lettering: Les Iris.

Madame Maigret guessed at the conflict going on inside him. He hadn't wanted to go to the police headquarters, just as right now he hadn't wanted to cross the street and tell the police officer who he was and gain admission to the house.

There wasn't a cloud in the sky. The street was clean, the air clear, light, joyful. A few houses further down, a woman was beating her carpets at the window, watching the spectators with a pitying look. But the previous day, when the murder had been discovered and the police had arrived in large numbers, hadn't she herself mingled with the neighbours to stare at a façade which she'd been familiar with for years?

Some exchanged opinions.

'Apparently it was a crime of passion . . .'

'Don't be ridiculous! She was nearly fifty . . .'

On the first floor, a face with dark hair and a pointed nose could be made out behind the windows, and sometimes in the background the shape of a man who was still young.

The door was white. A milk float went past, and bottles were deposited on most doorsteps. The milkman walked towards the white door holding a bottle of milk. The police officer said something to him, probably that there was no point, but the milkman shrugged and left the bottle anyway.

Was anyone going to notice that Maigret . . . ? He couldn't stay there indefinitely . . .

Just when he was about to set off again, a tall young man with a mop of hair appeared in the doorway, crossed the street and walked straight up to him.

'The chief superintendent would like you to come and see him . . .'

His wife managed to suppress a smile.

'Where should I wait for you?' she asked.

'In our usual spot, at the spring . . .'

Had he been recognized through the window? He crossed the road in a dignified manner, trying to put on a grumpy expression. The hallway was cool, and on the right was a bamboo coat rack where two hats hung. He added his, a straw boater which his wife had made him buy at the same time as the mohair jacket he was a little ashamed of.

'Come in, chief . . .'

A familiar, jovial voice, a face and a shape that Maigret recognized at once.

'Lecoeur!'

They hadn't seen each other for fifteen years, when Désiré Lecoeur, an inspector at the time, had still been part of Maigret's team at Quai des Orfèvres.

'Yes, chief, we gain experience, a paunch and stripes. Here I am, chief superintendent in Clermont-Ferrand, which is why I'm landed with this exasperating case . . . Come in . . .'

He showed him into a small sitting room blue with smoke and sat down at the table serving as a temporary desk, which was strewn with papers.

Maigret lowered himself gingerly on to a delicate Louis XVI chair and there must have been a questioning look in his eyes, because Lecoeur hastily said:

'You're probably wondering how I knew you were here? First of all, Moinet, whom you haven't met and who is head of the Vichy police, saw your name among the hotel index cards . . . Naturally, he didn't dare disturb you, but his men see you walk past every day . . . Apparently even the coastguards are wondering when you'll decide to play boules . . . Each morning, you seem to be more and more interested in the game, to the point—'

'Did you get here yesterday?'

'From Clermont-Ferrand, of course, with two of my men, including young Dicelle who brought you in from the street. I was loath to send him to fetch you. I said to myself that you're here to take the waters, not to give us a hand. I also knew that if you were intrigued by the case, you'd end up—'

Now Maigret really looked grumpy.

'A financially motivated murder?' he growled.

'Definitely not.'

'A crime of passion?'

'Unlikely. I say that, but, after twenty-four hours, I'm barely any the wiser than when I arrived yesterday morning . . .'

He rummaged among his papers.

'The victim's name is Hélène Lange. She was forty-eight and was born in Marsilly, about ten kilometres from La Rochelle. I telephoned Marsilly town hall and found out that for many years her mother, widowed young, ran a small haberdashery on Place de l'Église.

'She had two daughters, and Hélène, the eldest, took a shorthand-typing course in La Rochelle . . . Then for a time she worked in the offices of a ship-owner before leaving for Paris, after which there's no trace of her . . .

'She never applied for a copy of her birth certificate, which suggests she never married. Besides, her identity card states single . . .

'She had a sister six or seven years her junior who was a manicurist in La Rochelle. Like her elder sibling, she went to Paris, but she returned after ten or so years.

'She must have built up a tidy sum which allowed her to buy a hair salon, on Place d'Armes, which she still runs . . . I tried to telephone her . . . but I only spoke to an assistant who's looking after the salon while she's on holiday in the Balearic Islands . . . I sent a cable to her hotel to ask her to fly home immediately and I'm expecting her later today . . .

'This sister, Francine, isn't married either . . . The mother died eight years ago . . . We're not aware of any other family . . .'

Maigret, despite himself, had his professional countenance. Anyone would have thought that he was in charge of the investigation and that one of his colleagues was giving him a report in his office.

He missed having his pipes in front of him, which he was in the habit of fiddling with in such circumstances, the view over the Seine through the window, his sturdy armchair with a back he could lean against.

While Lecoeur was speaking he noticed two or three details, in particular that in this lounge that served as a living room there were photographs only of Hélène Lange. On a sideboard were pictures of her aged five or six, in a dress that was too long for her, a thin braid either side of her face.

On the wall, a larger portrait by a skilled photographer showed her aged around twenty, in a romantic pose, her gaze ethereal.

In a third, she was standing at the edge of the sea. She was wearing not a bathing-costume but a white dress fluttering towards the left in the breeze, like a flag, and she was holding a light-coloured, broad-brimmed hat in both hands.

'Do you know when and how the murder was committed?'

'It's hard to piece together the events . . . We've been working on it since yesterday morning, but we've barely made any progress . . .

'The day before yesterday, that is Monday evening, Hélène Lange had dinner alone in her kitchen. She washed the dishes, because we didn't find any dirty crockery, got dressed up and went out after switching off all the lights. If you want to know, she ate two soft-boiled eggs. She was wearing a mauve dress and a white woollen stole, as well as a hat that was also white . . .'

Maigret hesitated but finally couldn't resist the urge to announce:

'I know . . .'

'Have you already investigated?'

'No, but on Monday evening, I glimpsed her sitting in front of the bandstand where there was a concert playing . . .'

'You don't know when she left the park?'

'My wife and I moved on from there before nine thirty on our usual stroll . . .'

'Was she on her own?'

'She was always on her own.'

Lecoeur didn't try to hide his astonishment.

'Had you noticed her on other occasions?'

A smiling Maigret nodded.

'Why?'

'Here, we spend our time walking and, automatically, people look at one another. They also meet at the same times in the same places . . .'

'Do you have an idea?'

'About what?'

'About the kind of woman she was?'

'She certainly wasn't ordinary, that's all I know . . .'

'Right . . . I'll go on . . . two of the three first-floor bedrooms are rented out . . . The first is occupied by an engineer from Grenoble, a certain Maleski, and his wife . . . They left the house a few minutes after Mademoiselle Lange to go to the cinema and they only got back at half past eleven . . . All the shutters were closed, as usual, but light could be seen between the slats of those on the ground floor . . . Once in the hallway, they noticed that there was light coming from under the door of the lounge and from Mademoiselle Lange's bedroom, which is on the right—'

'Did they not hear anything?'

'Maleski didn't hear anything . . . His wife, although very uncertain, spoke of a murmur of voices . . . They went to bed almost immediately and nothing woke them until the next morning . . .

'The other lodger is called Madame Vireveau, a widow who lives in Rue Lamarck, in Paris . . . She's an imposing person in her early sixties, who comes to Vichy every year to shed a few kilos . . . It's the first time she's rented a room from Mademoiselle Lange . . . In previous years she stayed at a hotel . . .

'People say she used to lead a different lifestyle, that her husband was a wealthy man but was too generous, which has left her in difficult circumstances . . . In short, she's dripping with fake jewellery and talks like a character in a bad play . . . She went out at nine p.m . . . She saw no one and left the house in total darkness . . .'

'Does each lodger have their own key?'

'Yes . . . The Vireveau widow went to the Carlton bridge club, which she left just before midnight . . . She walked back, as usual . . . She doesn't have a car. The Maleskis have a little motor car but rarely use it during their stay in Vichy and most of the time it's kept in a local garage . . .'

'Were the lights still on?'

'Hold on, chief . . . Of course, I wasn't able to question the Vireveau woman until after the murder had been discovered and the whole street was in turmoil . . . I don't know if her imagination is as colourful as her taste in costume jewellery . . . She claims that on reaching the corner of the street, in other words the intersection of Boulevard de La Salle and Rue du Bourbonnais, she almost bumped into a man . . . He hadn't been able to see her coming and she swears he was startled, and raised his hand to his face as if to avoid being recognized—'

'But she recognized him anyway!'

'No. She states that she'd be able to identify him all the same if she were to meet him face to face . . . He was very tall and very strong . . . A broad gorilla's chest, she says . . .

He was walking fast, leaning forwards . . . She was frightened, but she still turned around to look at him as he hurried on his way into town . . .'

'A man of what age?'

'Not young . . . Not old either . . . Very strong . . . Terrifying . . . She almost ran and only felt safe once the key was in the lock . . .'

'Were lights still visible on the ground floor?'

'That's the point, they were off, insofar as we can trust her testimony. She didn't hear anything. She went to bed, so upset that she took a spoonful of peppermint spirit on a sugar lump . . .'

'Who discovered the murder?'

'I'll get to that, chief. Mademoiselle Lange wanted to rent out her rooms to respectable people, but she wasn't prepared to provide meals . . . Nor did she allow them to cook, or even permit them to use a little spirit stove to make coffee in the morning . . .

'At around eight o'clock yesterday morning, Madame Maleski came downstairs with her Thermos to fill it with coffee at a nearby café and buy croissants, as she did every day . . . She didn't notice anything out of the ordinary . . . Nor when she returned . . . What surprised her was not hearing any noise, especially the second time, because Mademoiselle Lange usually rose early and could be heard moving from one room to the next . . .

' "I wonder whether she's ill," she said to her husband while they ate.

'Because the landlady was always complaining about her health. At nine o'clock, the couple went downstairs, whereas Madame Vireveau was still in her room and, in the hallway, they found Charlotte dumbstruck—'

'Charlotte?'

'A little servant girl whom Mademoiselle Lange employed every morning from nine to twelve to clean the rooms . . . She cycles over from a village around ten kilometres away and she's a bit simple . . .

' "All the doors are locked," she said to the Maleskis.

'On the other mornings, by the time she arrived, the ground-floor doors and windows were open because Mademoiselle Lange always said she needed some fresh air.

' "Don't you have the key?"

' "No . . . If she's not there, I may as well go home . . ."

'Maleski tried to open the door with the key to his room but wasn't able to, and in the end he called the police, from the same bar where his wife had just gone to get the coffee.

'That's about all. The Vichy police lieutenant soon arrived with a locksmith. The key to the lounge door was missing. The other doors, that of the kitchen and the bedroom, were locked . . .'

'In this lounge, here to be precise, on the edge of the rug, Hélène Lange was lying, or rather she was curled up, and she wasn't a pretty sight because she'd been strangled . . .

'She was still wearing her mauve dress, but she'd taken off her stole and hat, which we found on the coat-stand in the hall . . . The various drawers were open and papers and cardboard boxes were scattered over the floor—'

'No rape?'

'Not even attempted . . . Nothing stolen either, as far as we can tell . . . The report in this morning's *La Tribune* is quite accurate . . . In a drawer we found five one-hundred-franc notes . . . The victim's handbag had been searched, its contents strewn on the floor like the rest, including four hundred francs in ten- and twenty-franc notes as well as some small change and a season ticket for the Grand Casino theatre.'

'How long ago did she buy this house?'

'Nine years . . . She moved here from Nice, where she lived for a while . . .'

'Did she work there?'

'No . . . She lived in a modest apartment near Boulevard Albert-1er, and seemed to be a woman of independent means . . .'

'Did she travel?'

'Two- or three-day trips, practically every month . . .'

'Does anyone know where she went?'

'She was secretive about her comings and goings . . .'

'What about here?'

'The first two years, she didn't take in lodgers . . . Then she rented out three rooms during the season, but all three weren't always occupied . . . That's the case at present . . . The blue room is empty . . . Because there's the white room, the pink room and the blue room . . .'

Maigret noticed something else. He could not see a single touch of green, not an ornament, not a cushion or decoration.

'Was she superstitious?'

'How do you know? One day, she lost her temper because Madame Maleski had bought a bunch of carnations and she told her that she didn't want those unlucky flowers in the house . . .

'Again, she told Madame Vireveau that she was unwise to wear a green dress and that it would undoubtedly cost her dear . . .'

'Did she have any visitors?'

'Never, according to the neighbours.'

'Post?'

'From time to time, a letter from La Rochelle. The postman has been questioned. Flyers. Bills from some shops in Vichy.'

'Did she have a bank account?'

'At the Crédit Lyonnais, on the corner of Rue Georges-Clemenceau.'

'You've been there, of course?'

'She paid in regular amounts, around five thousand francs every month, not always on the same date.'

'In cash?'

'Yes . . . During the season, she deposited more, because of the rent from her lodgers—'

'Did she ever write cheques?'

'To shops, nearly all in Vichy or Moulins, where she would go occasionally . . . Sometimes she paid by cheque for items she bought from Paris by mail order . . . You'll find a pile of catalogues in this corner . . .'

Lecoeur watched Maigret, whose cream jacket made him look very different from the man he knew from Quai des Orfèvres.

'What do you reckon, chief?'

'That I have to go . . . My wife's waiting for me . . .'

'And your first glass of water!'

'The Vichy police know that too?' he grumbled.

'Will you come back? The Police Judiciaire doesn't have an office in Vichy. Every night I drive back to Clermont-Ferrand, which is only sixty kilometres away. The police chief here has offered to put a room and a telephone at my disposal, but I prefer to work at the scene . . . My men are trying to find passers-by or neighbours who might have seen Mademoiselle Lange on Monday evening, when she returned home, because we don't know whether there was someone with her or whether she met someone in the street or whether—'

'I'm sorry, my friend . . . my wife . . .'

'Of course, chief . . .'

Maigret was torn between his curiosity and his routine. He was a little annoyed with himself for having turned right instead of left on leaving the Hôtel de la Bérézina. He'd have paused as he did every morning at the children's playground, then, further on, he'd have watched the boules players.

Had Madame Maigret gone on their daily promenade alone, stopping at each of their usual places?

'Wouldn't you like a lift? My car's outside and young Dicelle would be only too happy to—'

'No thank you . . . I'm here to walk . . .'

And he walked, alone, striding quickly to make up for lost time.

He had drunk his first glass of water and found his usual spot, between the vast glazed Fountain Hall and the first tree. He could sense that, although his wife didn't ask him any questions, she was alert to his every gesture and facial expression.

His newspaper on his knee, he gazed up at the sky through the barely trembling foliage. It was the same clear blue as always, with one small, drifting, dazzling white cloud.

In Paris, he sometimes complained that he missed certain sensations for which he was nostalgic: a breath of air, warmed by the sunshine on his cheek, the play of light among the leaves or on the gravel crunching beneath the feet of the crowd, and even the taste of dust.

Here, a miracle happened. As he mulled over his conversation with Lecoeur, he felt as if he was immersed in the atmosphere, and nothing that was going on around him escaped him.

Was he really thinking? Was he daydreaming? Families strolled past, as everywhere, but there were many more older couples.

Were there more lone men or lone women? The women, especially the elderly ones, tended to gather in groups. You could see them arranging the chairs in circles of six or eight, and they'd lean towards one another and appear to be exchanging secrets, even though they'd only met a few days earlier.

Who knows? Maybe they were real secrets. They talked about their aches and pains, their doctor, their therapy, and then about their married offspring and their grandchildren, whisking photos from their handbags.

It was rare to see one sitting alone like the lady in lilac whose name he now knew.

It was more usual to see lone men, their faces often haunted by weariness or disease, struggling to make their way through the crowds with dignity. All the same, their features, their eyes, betrayed a sort of anxiety, a vague fear of collapsing in a pool of shade or sunlight amid the legs of the passers-by.

Hélène Lange was a loner and her attitude, her bearing, exuded a sort of pride. She didn't want to be called a spinster, did not accept pity, she held herself upright and walked with a light tread, her chin high.

She mixed with no one, had no need to unburden her soul or her mind by confiding in casual acquaintances.

Had she chosen to live alone? he wondered, intrigued. He tried to picture her sitting, standing, motionless, moving about.

'Do they have any leads?'

Madame Maigret was beginning to be jealous of his reverie. In Paris, she would not have dared ask her husband any questions midway through an investigation. But here, walking side by side for hours, had they not got into the habit of thinking aloud?

It was never a real conversation, an exchange of precise rejoinders, but nearly always a few words or a comment that was enough to indicate the other person's train of thought.

'No. They're waiting for the sister . . .'

'She doesn't have any other family?'

'Apparently not . . .'

'It's time for your second glass.'

They went inside the Fountain Hall where the attendants'

heads were visible above the sunken bar behind which they worked. Hélène Lange used to come and drink here every day. Was it on doctor's orders or simply to give herself a purpose for her walk?

'What are you thinking about?'

'I'm asking myself, why Vichy?'

She'd moved to this town around ten years ago and bought a house. So she was thirty-seven at the time and did not appear to need to earn a living because, in the first two years, she hadn't rented out the first-floor bedrooms.

'And why not?' retorted Madame Maigret.

'There are hundreds of small and medium-sized towns in France where she could have moved to, not to mention La Rochelle, which she knew from her childhood and adolescence . . . Her sister, after living in Paris, went back to La Rochelle and settled down there . . .'

'Maybe the two sisters didn't get along?'

It wasn't so straightforward. Maigret was still watching the people walking, and their pace reminded him of a similar permanent procession elsewhere, in the warm sunshine. In Nice, on the Promenade des Anglais.

Because, before coming to Vichy, Hélène Lange had lived in Nice for five years.

'She lived in Nice for five years,' he said aloud.

'A lot of people with small private incomes . . .'

'Quite . . . People with small private incomes, but also people from every walk of life, just like here . . . I was wondering the day before yesterday what the crowds strolling in this park and sitting on the chairs reminded

43

me of . . . It's the same as on the seafront in Nice . . .
Crowds from so many different backgrounds that they
become neutral . . . Here too there must be former stage
and screen celebrities . . . We discovered a neighbourhood
of opulent mansions where you can still glimpse men-
servants in striped waistcoats . . .

'In the hills, you can make out luxurious, secluded
villas . . .

'Like in Nice . . .'

'What do you infer from that?'

'Nothing. She was thirty-two when she moved to Nice
and she was as alone there as she was here. In general,
solitude sets in later . . .'

'There is such a thing as heartache . . .'

'I know, but it doesn't cause a face like that.'

'There are also broken relationships . . .'

'Ninety-five per cent of women remarry.'

'What about men?'

He gave her a broad smile and said, without her real-
izing that he was joking:

'One hundred per cent!'

In Nice, there was a floating population, branches of
Paris shops and several casinos. In Vichy, tens of thousands of people came to take the waters, changing every
three weeks, and there were the same shops, three casinos and a dozen cinemas.

Anywhere else, she would have been known, people
would have gossiped about her and spied on her.

Not in Nice. Not in Vichy. So did she have something
to hide?

'Do you have to meet up with Lecoeur?'

'He invited me to drop by and see him when I want . . . He still calls me chief like when he was in my department . . .'

'They all do . . .'

'It's true . . . Out of habit . . .'

'You don't think it's more out of affection?'

He shrugged, and they soon found themselves making their way back to their hotel. This time they went through the old town, pausing in front of the poignant displays in the windows of the antiques shops.

They knew that, at mealtimes, the other guests watched them, but they had to get used to it. Maigret tried to follow Doctor Rian's recommendations. Chew every mouthful carefully before swallowing, even mashed potatoes. Don't pick up more food on your fork before you've swallowed the previous mouthful. Don't drink more than one or two sips of water, possibly tinted with a dash of wine . . .

He preferred no wine at all.

He indulged in a few puffs on his pipe before going upstairs and lying down fully dressed for his nap. Enough light filtered through the shutters for his wife, in the armchair, to take her turn at skimming the newspaper, and, through his drowsiness, he could hear a rustle as she turned the page.

He had been lying down for barely twenty minutes when there was a knock on the door. Madame Maigret scuttled out on to the landing and closed the door behind her. There was whispering, then she went downstairs, and was only out of the room for a few minutes.

'That was Lecoeur.'

'Has there been a development?'

'The sister's just arrived in Vichy. She went to the police station and they're going to drive her to the morgue to identify the body. Lecoeur's waiting for her at Rue du Bourbonnais. He wondered whether you'd like to go over there and be present when he questions her.'

Maigret was already on his feet, grumbling, and he began by opening the shutters to bring light and life back into the room.

'Shall I meet you at the spring?'

The spring, the first glass of water, the iron chair, weren't until five o'clock in the afternoon.

'It won't take that long. Wait for me on one of the benches near the boules players instead . . .'

He wasn't sure whether to take his straw hat.

'Are you afraid they'll laugh at you?'

Too bad. He was on holiday, after all, and he placed it proudly on his head.

Curious bystanders continued to stop in front of the house, still under police guard. Once they realized that there was nothing to see except closed windows, they soon moved off, shaking their heads.

'Have a seat, chief . . . If you place the chair in the corner, near the window, you'll see her in the full light . . .'

'Haven't you met her yet?'

'I was having lunch – in an excellent restaurant incidentally – when I was informed that she was at the police station . . . She's being taken to the morgue and then brought to me.'

Through the net curtains, they spotted a black vehicle, driven by a uniformed police officer, followed by a long red open-topped car. The couple in the front, hair dishevelled, faces tanned, looked very much as if they were returning home from a holiday.

The woman and the man exchanged a few words then leaned towards each other and, after a quick kiss, the woman got out and slammed the door, while her companion remained at the wheel and lit a cigarette.

He was swarthy, with clearly defined features and muscles rippling beneath his yellow polo shirt. He looked in the direction of the house without curiosity as the police officer showed the young woman into the lounge.

'Detective Chief Inspector Lecoeur . . . You are Francine Lange, I assume?'

'That's correct . . .'

She glanced vaguely over at Maigret, who was not introduced to her and sat with his back to the light.

'Madame or mademoiselle?'

'I'm not married, if that's what you mean. My friend, who's in the car, is with me. But I know men too well to marry one. Afterwards, they're a nightmare to get rid of . . .'

She was an attractive woman who didn't look her forty years as she paraded her provocative figure around the small conventional lounge. She wore a flame-coloured dress, so light that it was see-through, and you could have sworn she gave off a whiff of the sea.

'The telegram reached me last night . . . Lucien managed to get us seats on the first flight to Paris . . . At Orly, we picked up our car, which we'd left there when we flew out—'

'I presume that the victim is indeed your sister?'

She nodded, without emotion.

'Wouldn't you like to sit down?'

'Thank you. May I smoke?'

She watched the smoke rising from Maigret's pipe as if to say: 'If he can sit there puffing away, then I should be allowed a cigarette.'

'Please do . . . I imagine this murder is as much of a shock to you as it is to us?'

'It's the last thing I'd have expected . . .'

'Do you know if your sister had any enemies?'

'Why would Hélène have any enemies?'

'When was the last time you saw her?'

'Six or seven years ago. I don't know exactly . . . I remember that it was in winter and there was a storm . . . She hadn't told me she was coming, and I was surprised to see her walk calmly into my hair salon.'

'Did you get along with her?'

'As sisters do . . . I didn't know her that well because of the age gap . . . She left school when I was just starting . . . Then she took lessons in La Rochelle. That was a long time before I became a manicurist . . . After that she moved away—'

'How old was she then?'

'Hold on . . . I'd been doing my apprenticeship for a year . . . So I was sixteen . . . Add seven . . . She was twenty-three.'

'Did you write to her?'

'Rarely . . . Our family's not the sort . . .'

'Was your mother already dead?'

'No . . . She died two years later and Hélène came to Marsilly for the division of the inheritance . . . There wasn't a lot to divide up . . . The shop wasn't worth a great deal . . .'

'What did your sister do in Paris?'

Maigret continued to scrutinize her, while recalling the shape and face of the dead woman. The two siblings had little in common, and Francine did not have her sister's long face or her dark eyes. Hers were blue and her hair was blond, perhaps dyed, because she had a curious strand of flaming auburn in the front.

At first glance, she was a hardworking woman who doubtless greeted her customers with cheerful, even saucy good humour. She didn't try to appear sophisticated, on the contrary, it was as if she delighted in flaunting her vulgar side.

Less than half an hour after viewing her sister's body at the morgue, she sounded almost cheerful as she answered the questions put to her by Lecoeur, on whom it appeared she was working her charm, out of habit.

'What did she do in Paris? . . . I suppose she was a typist in an office, but I never went to see her there . . . We were very different, the two of us . . . At fifteen, I already had a boyfriend, who was a taxi-driver, and since then I've had lots of others . . . I don't think Hélène was like that, or if she was she kept it quiet . . .'

'What address did you write to her at?'

'I remember, at first, a hotel in Avenue de Clichy, but

I've forgotten the name . . . She changed lodgings quite often . . . Then she had an apartment in Rue Notre-Dame-de-Lorette, I don't recall the number . . .'

'And when you went to Paris as well, didn't you visit her?'

'Oh yes, I did . . . It was in Rue Notre-Dame-de-Lorette, and I was amazed to see her living somewhere so classy . . . I said so to her . . . She had a lovely bedroom overlooking the street, a living room, a kitchenette and a proper bathroom . . .'

'Was there a man in her life?'

'I wasn't able to find out . . . I wanted to stay with her for a few days until I found a suitable room, but she said she'd take me to lodgings that were very clean and inexpensive, because she couldn't live with anyone . . .'

'Not even for three or four days?'

'That's what I understood.'

'Did that not surprise you?'

'Not particularly . . . You know, it takes a lot to surprise me . . . So long as people let me do what I want, they're free too and I don't ask any questions . . .'

'How long did you stay in Paris?'

'Eleven years . . .'

'As a manicurist all that time?'

'At first, in local hair salons, then, towards the end, in a luxury hotel on the Champs-Élysées . . . I trained to become a beautician . . .'

'Did you live alone?'

'Sometimes alone, sometimes not . . .'

'Did you use to meet up with your sister?'

'Almost never . . .'

'So you know very little of her life in Paris?'

'All I know is that she worked . . .'

'When you returned to La Rochelle to set up on your own, did you have a lot of savings?'

'Enough . . .'

He didn't ask her how she had earned that money. She wasn't forthcoming on the subject either, but it seemed that they understood each other.

'You never married?'

'I've already told you, I'm not so stupid . . .'

And, turning towards the window, through which her companion could be seen, posing at the wheel of his red car:

'See how sly he looks . . .'

'But even so, you live with him . . .'

'He works for me and is an excellent hairdresser to boot . . . In La Rochelle, we live separately, because I don't want him underfoot day and night . . . On holiday, it's all right . . .'

'Are you the owner of the car?'

'Of course.'

'Did he choose it?'

'You guessed . . .'

'Did your sister ever have any children?'

'Why are you asking me that?'

'I don't know . . . She was a woman . . .'

'As far as I know, she didn't . . . I'd have thought we'd have known, wouldn't we?'

'What about you?'

'I had a baby when I was still living in Paris, fifteen years ago . . . At first I wanted to get rid of it, and it would have been better . . . It was my sister who advised me to keep it . . .'

'So you saw each other at that time?'

'I went to see her because of that . . . I needed to talk about it with someone in the family . . . It might sound funny, but there are times you remember you have a family . . . In short, I had a son, Philippe . . . I sent him to be fostered in the Vosges . . .'

'Why the Vosges? Do you have any connections there?'

'Not at all. Hélène found the address in some newspaper . . . I went to see him a dozen or so times in two years . . . He was fine, being cared for by a very kind farming couple . . . Their place was clean . . . Then, one fine day, they told me that the little boy had drowned in the pond . . .'

She looked wistful for a moment, then shrugged.

'After all, maybe it was the best thing for him . . .'

'You've never met any friends of your sister's, either male or female?'

'She couldn't have had many. Already, in Marsilly, she thought she was better than the other girls and they called her "the princess". I think it was the same at the shorthand-typing school, in La Rochelle . . .'

'Was she proud?'

She hesitated, thinking.

'I don't know. That's not the word I'd use. She didn't like people. She didn't like socializing with people. That's it! She preferred her own company . . .'

'Did she ever attempt suicide?'

'Why? Do you think . . . ?'

Lecoeur smiled.

'No . . . You don't commit suicide by strangling your-self . . . I simply wonder whether, in the past, she was ever tempted to end her life . . .'

'I'm certain she didn't . . . She was happy with the way she was . . . Deep down, she was very self-satisfied . . .'

The word struck Maigret and he pictured the lady in lilac sitting in front of the bandstand. He'd tried then to define the expression on her face but hadn't found the right word.

Francine had just done so: she was perfectly happy with herself!

She loved herself so much that in her lounge there were three photographs of her, and there were probably more in the dining room and bedroom, which they hadn't searched. No one else. No portrait of her mother, her sister, male or female friends. By the sea, she'd had her photograph taken alone beside the waves.

'For the time being, I assume you are her only heir . . . We haven't found a will among her papers . . . It's true that the murderer scattered documents everywhere, but I don't see why he'd have stolen a will . . . No notary has come forward—'

'When's the funeral?'

'That's up to you . . . The coroner has finished with the body, which can be handed over to you as soon as you wish . . .'

'Where do you think I should bury her?'

'I have no idea.'

'I don't know anyone here . . . In Marsilly, the entire village would come to the funeral, out of curiosity . . . I wonder whether she'd have liked to go back to Marsilly . . . Look, if you don't need me any more, I'll go and find a hotel room had have a nice, long bath, because I need to . . . I'll try to think and, tomorrow morning . . .'

'I'll expect you tomorrow morning, then . . .'

As she left, having shaken Lecoeur's hand, she turned to Maigret for a moment, as if wondering what he was doing there, sitting silently in his corner, and then she frowned.

Had she recognized him?

'See you tomorrow . . . You have been very kind . . .'

They saw her get into the car and lean over to her companion to say a few words, and then the car drove off.

In the lounge the two men exchanged glances, and Lecoeur was the first to blurt out, almost comically:

'Well?'

To which Maigret replied, puffing on his pipe:

'Yes! Well?'

He didn't feel like talking and hadn't forgotten he was meeting his wife near the boules players.

'See you tomorrow, my friend . . .'

'See you tomorrow . . .'

As he left, he was honoured with a military salute from the officer standing guard, but that didn't make him feel especially proud.

3.

Once again, he was sitting in the green armchair close to the open window. The weather was the same as when they had arrived, glorious hot sunshine yet cool air in the mornings when the municipal cleaning trucks drove up and down the streets. It was cool too during the day, beneath the trees that were everywhere – in the park, along the riverbank and lining the many avenues.

He had eaten his three croissants. His cup of coffee was still half full. His wife, next door, was running a bath and he could hear the footsteps of the guests on the floor above who had just risen.

It was not without irony that he was slipping so easily into these new habits. Wherever he was, he inevitably created a routine which he obeyed as if he had no choice.

It could be said that each of his investigations in Paris had its own pace, with its pauses in particular cafés and bars, particular smells and particular quality of light.

Here, he felt more as if he was on holiday than undergoing treatment, and the death of the lady in lilac was set against a backdrop of idleness.

The previous evening, like the other evenings, they had gone for a stroll in the park, where hundreds of visitors like them moved from the shade into the light shed by the frosted-glass spheres. It was the hour of theatres, casinos and cinemas. People came out of their hotels, boarding houses or lodgings where they'd eaten cold meats, and they were all hurrying to their chosen entertainment.

Many were content to sit on the yellow iron chairs with their romantic curves, and Maigret had automatically looked for the upright, dignified form, with her long face, high chin and gaze that was both nostalgic and steely.

Hélène Lange was dead and, in a hotel room, Francine was probably discussing with her gigolo where her sister was to be buried.

Somewhere in the town, a man had the key to the mystery of Les Iris and the solitary woman: the man who had strangled her.

Was he still out walking in the park or was he on his way to a theatre or cinema right now?

Maigret and his wife had gone to bed without talking about it, but they both knew that it was on the other's mind.

He lit his pipe and turned the page of his newspaper to find the local news. He frowned on seeing a photograph of himself splashed over two columns, a shot he'd never seen, taken without his knowledge when he was drinking one of his daily glasses of water. Beside him, about a third of his wife's form was visible, and, behind him, two or three anonymous faces.

MAIGRET TO INVESTIGATE?

Out of discretion, we had not informed our readers of the presence among us of Detective Chief Inspector Maigret, who is in Vichy not on a case but to enjoy, like so many other illustrious figures before him, the therapeutic benefits of our waters.

But will the inspector be able to resist the urge to elucidate the mystery of Rue du Bourbonnais?

Reportedly he was seen outside the house where the murder took place and is even said to be in contact with the affable Detective Chief Inspector Lecoeur, head of the Clermont-Ferrand Police Judiciaire, who is in charge of the investigation.

Will Inspector Maigret give priority to his treatment or . . .

He threw down the newspaper, without anger, because he was used to this kind of rumour, shrugged and stared vaguely out of the window.

Until nine o'clock, his movements were the same as on the other mornings and when Madame Maigret appeared, in a pink suit, they made their way quite naturally downstairs.

'Have a good day, Monsieur Maigret, Madame . . .'

That was the owner's inevitable morning send-off. Maigret had already spotted two figures on the pavement, the glint of a camera lens.

'They've been waiting for you for an hour . . . It's not the ones from *La Montagne*, where you were mentioned this morning, they're from *La Tribune*, from Saint-Étienne . . .'

The man with the camera was a tall redhead, the other was short and dark with one shoulder higher than the other. They raced over to the entrance.

'May we take a photo, just one?'

What was the point of saying no? He stood still for a moment between the two shrubs either side of the main door, while Madame Maigret retreated to the shadows.

'Lift your head up a little, because of the hat . . .'

This was the first time in ages that he'd been snapped wearing a straw hat, and he only wore one in Meung-sur-Loire, an old gardener's hat.

'Just one more . . . Just a second shot . . . Thank you . . .'

'Monsieur Maigret, may I ask you if you really are handling the case . . . ?'

'As head of the Crime Squad at Quai des Orfèvres, it is not my job to get involved with investigations outside Paris . . .'

'But you're interested in this murder, aren't you?'

'As are most of your readers . . .'

'Does it not present a rather unusual character?'

'I don't understand what you mean.'

'The victim was a loner . . . She didn't socialize at all . . . There doesn't appear to be any motive to—'

'When we know more about her, the motive will probably become clear . . .'

It was a noncommittal answer that didn't compromise him in any way. All the same, it contained a truth. Maigret was not the only one who'd been seeking for a long time to learn about murder victims' characters. Criminologists were attaching a growing importance to the dead person, even going so far, in many cases, as to place a large share of the blame on them.

Was there not, in the life and behaviour of Hélène Lange, something that predestined her somehow to die a violent death? The moment he first set eyes on her in the shady park, she had intrigued Maigret.

True, others, like the merry couple, had also caught his eye.

'Wasn't Inspector Lecoeur once part of your team?'

'He used to work for the Police Judiciaire in Paris.'

'Have you seen him?'

'Only to say hello to.'

'Will you see him again?'

'Very likely.'

'Will you discuss the murder with him?'

'Possibly. Unless we discuss the weather and the special quality of the light in your town . . .'

'What's special about it?'

'A certain shimmer, a certain softness . . .'

'Do you plan to come back to Vichy next year?'

'That depends on my doctor.'

'Thank you.'

They both jumped into an old car, while Maigret and his wife walked a few paces along the street.

'Where shall I wait for you?'

That implied that her husband intended to go to Rue du Bourbonnais.

'At the spring?'

'At the boules game . . .'

In other words, he didn't plan to stay with Lecoeur for long. He found him in the cramped lounge, busy on the telephone.

'Have a seat, chief . . . Hello! . . . Yes . . . It's lucky the concierge has stayed in the job for so many years . . .

Yes . . . She doesn't know where . . . ? She took the Métro . . . ? Yes, at Saint-Georges . . . Don't hang up, mademoiselle . . . Go on, my friend . . .'

The conversation continued for another two or three minutes.

'Thank you. I'll send you a formal letter of request so that everything is in order . . . Then you can send me your report . . . Your wife . . . ? Of course . . . Kids are always a worry . . . Don't I know it, with my four boys . . .'

He hung up and turned to Maigret.

'That was Julien, whom you must know and who's currently an inspector in the ninth arrondissement . . . I asked him yesterday to rummage around in the files and he found Hélène Lange's exact address in Rue Notre-Dame-de-Lorette, where she lived for four years—'

'So from the age of twenty-eight to thirty-two . . .'

'That's correct . . . The concierge is still there . . . Mademoiselle Lange was reportedly a quiet young woman . . . She kept regular hours, like a person who works . . . She went out rarely in the evenings, to go to the theatre or the cinema apparently . . .

'Her office can't have been in the neighbourhood, because she took the Métro . . . She went out and did her shopping early, and she didn't have a cleaner . . . At around twelve twenty, she'd come home for lunch and would leave at one thirty . . . Then she'd return home again at half past six.'

'She didn't have any visitors?'

'A man, just one, and always the same.'

'Does the concierge happen to know his name?'

'She knows nothing about him. He only came once or twice a week, at around eight thirty, and he always left at ten o'clock . . .'

'What sort?'

'A respectable man, apparently. He had a car. It never occurred to the concierge to write down the registration number. A large black sedan, probably American . . .'

'How old?'

'Around forty . . . Quite stout . . . Very elegant, very well dressed . . .'

'Was it he who paid the rent?'

'He never went into the lodge . . .'

'Did they go away for the weekend together?'

'Once.'

'On holiday?'

'No . . . At that time, Hélène Lange only took two weeks' holiday and every year she went to Étretat, where she had her post forwarded to a family boarding house . . .'

'Did she receive a lot of mail?'

'Very little . . . The occasional letter from her sister . . . She had a subscription to a local bookshop and she read a lot . . .'

'Can I look around the apartment?'

'Make yourself at home, chief . . .'

He noticed that the television wasn't in the lounge but in the Provençal-style dining room with a lot of shiny brass pots. On the dresser stood a photo of Hélène Lange playing with a hoop, and another of her posing in a swimsuit in front of a cliff, most likely at Étretat. She had a good figure, slender, like her face, but not skinny, not withered.

She was one of those women likely to be misjudged when dressed up.

The modern, cheerful kitchen had a dishwasher and all the appliances that make the housewife's life easier.

The rooms led off from the hallway, and Maigret found himself in a bathroom that was also modern, and finally in the dead woman's bedroom.

He was amused to find the same brass bedstead as at the hotel, and almost the same ornate furniture. The striped wallpaper was pale pink and mauvy-blue and here too was a photograph showing Hélène Lange, aged around thirty.

Her expression was very different, and her spontaneous, open smile exuded joie de vivre.

It was an enlarged Polaroid, and a background of foliage suggested it had been taken in a wood. She was gazing into the camera with a certain affection.

'I'd be curious to know who was taking the photograph,' muttered Maigret to Lecoeur, who had joined him.

'Strange girl, wasn't she?'

'I presume you've questioned the lodgers?'

'It also occurred to me that the murder could have been committed by someone in the house. The widow's out of the frame because, despite her bulk, she's not strong enough to strangle someone as resilient as Mademoiselle Lange . . . We checked the Carlton, where she was indeed playing bridge until eleven twenty . . . Whereas, according to the coroner, the murder must have been committed between ten and eleven p.m . . .'

'In other words, when Madame Vireveau got home, Hélène Lange was already dead.'

'That is almost certain.'

'The Maleskis saw a light under the lounge door . . . Since the lights were out when the body was found, the murderer must still have been in the house . . .'

'I keep saying to myself . . . either he came in with his victim and strangled her before ransacking the room, or she caught him in the act and he suffocated her . . .'

'What about the man Madame Vireveau claims to have bumped into on the street corner?'

'We're working on it . . . At around that time, a bar owner who was lowering his metal shutter saw a corpulent individual walking hurriedly . . . He states that the man sounded out of breath . . .'

'In which direction?'

'Towards Les Célestins . . .'

'No description?'

'He didn't take any notice . . . All he knows is that he was wearing dark clothes and was hatless . . . He thinks he recalls that he had a receding hairline . . .'

'No anonymous letters?'

'Not yet . . .'

There would be. No case shrouded in mystery ends without the police receiving a number of anonymous letters and furtive telephone calls.

'You haven't seen the sister again?'

'I'm waiting for her instructions as to what to do with the body . . .'

He added after a silence:

'The two sisters are as different as chalk and cheese, aren't they? While one appears to have been reserved and withdrawn, with a certain disdain for everything around her, the other embraces life, exudes health . . . And yet . . .'

Maigret smiled as he looked at Lecoeur who, with the passing years, had indeed developed a paunch and had a few white hairs in his auburn moustache. His blue eyes were innocent, almost childlike, yet Maigret remembered him as one of his best colleagues.

'Why are you smiling?'

'Because I saw her alive, and from her photos and what you've been told about her, you have drawn the same conclusions as I have . . .'

'Hélène Lange was a fake sentimentalist, a fake romantic, wasn't she?'

'I believe she was playing a part, possibly for herself, but she couldn't help her eyes being hard and sharp . . .'

'Like her sister . . .'

'Francine Lange, on the other hand, plays the liberated woman, the girl who's afraid of nothing, who doesn't give a damn what people think . . . In La Rochelle, I'm sure she's a well-loved character whose hijinks are the subject of gossip . . .'

'Which doesn't stop her, from occasionally . . .'

They didn't need to finish their sentences.

'She's no fool!'

'And she knows what she wants, irrespective of all the gigolos on earth . . . Starting out from a little shop in Marsilly, now, at forty, she's the owner of one of the biggest hair salons in La Rochelle . . . I know the town, and Place d'Armes . . .'

He took his watch out of his pocket.

'My wife's waiting for me . . .'

'At the spring?'

'First of all, I'm going to clear my mind and watch the boules game . . . I tried playing once, in Porquerolles . . . If those gentlemen twist my arm . . .'

He walked off, filling a new pipe, and found the air much warmer. He was glad to be back in the shade of the big trees.

'Any news?'

'Nothing of interest . . .'

'They still know nothing of her life in Paris?'

His wife watched him for signs she should stop asking questions, but she felt emboldened by his cheerful mood.

'Nothing precise . . . Only that she once had a lover . . .'

'You sound happy about that . . .'

'Perhaps . . . It suggests that at one point in her life at least she had a good time . . . She hasn't always been withdrawn, brooding over heaven knows what notions or dreams . . .'

'What's known about him?'

'Almost nothing, except that he drove a big black car, that he came to see her only once or twice a week, that he left before ten o'clock at night and they never spent the holidays or weekends together.'

'A married man . . .'

'Most likely . . . Around forty . . . Ten years older than her . . .'

'Didn't the residents of Rue du Bourbonnais ever see him?'

'First of all, he's no longer forty . . . He must be getting on for sixty, if not more—'

'Do you think—'

'I don't think anything . . . I'd like to know how she lived in Nice, whether there was a transition or whether she behaved like a spinster as she did here . . . Watch . . . He's going to shoot the jack out . . .'

It was the one-armed player, who took his time, shot his boule and sent the wooden jack flying on to the lawn.

'I envy them . . .' he couldn't help muttering.

'Why?'

He thought she looked younger, with the interplay of light and shadow on her smooth face. Her eyes were shining. He felt as if he was on holiday again.

'Haven't you noticed their attitude, their air of importance, the expression of intense satisfaction when they pull off a good shot . . . ? Whereas when we wrap up an investigation . . .'

He broke off mid-sentence, but the expression on his face said it all. They sent a man to court, to prison, or sometimes to his death.

He stopped and said, after emptying his pipe:

'Shall we walk?'

Wasn't that why they were there?

Lecoeur's colleagues had questioned all the neighbours. Not only had no one seen or heard anything on the night of the murder, but they were all unanimous in asserting that Hélène Lange had no friends, male or female, and that she never received any visitors.

'Sometimes she goes away, carrying a little holdall, and the shutters stay closed for two or three days.'

She never took a bigger suitcase. She had no car and did not call a taxi.

Nor did anyone ever run into her in the street in the company of another person, man or woman.

In the mornings, she'd go out to the local shops. She wasn't especially stingy, but she knew the value of money and on Saturdays she'd go to the big market to buy food, always wearing a white hat in summer, a dark one in the winter.

As for her current lodgers, they were in the clear. Madame Vireveau had rented a room on the recommendation of a friend from Montmartre who had stayed with Mademoiselle Lange for several seasons. Although she was quite conspicuous because of her stoutness and her fake jewellery, she wasn't the sort to murder someone, especially without a motive. Her husband had been a florist and up until his death she'd helped him in his shop on Boulevard des Batignolles, before retiring to a small apartment in Rue Lamarck.

'I have nothing against her,' she said of Hélène Lange, 'except that she wasn't talkative.'

The Maleskis had been taking the waters at Vichy for four years. The first year, they'd stayed in a hotel and on one of their walks they'd noticed a sign advertising a room to rent in Rue du Bourbonnais. They inquired about the price and booked the room for the following summer. This was their third season in the house.

Maleski suffered from liver disease, which forced him

to take things easy and to follow a strict regimen. At forty-two he was already a lacklustre man with a sad smile, which did not prevent him from being, according to witness statements gathered over the telephone from Grenoble, a valuable professional and of scrupulous conscience.

He and his wife had realized from the first year that Mademoiselle Lange did not wish to be on friendly terms with her lodgers. They'd only been into the lounge two or three times and were not acquainted with the other rooms on the ground floor. She had never invited them in for a drink or a cup of coffee.

On rainy days, in the evenings, they sometimes heard the television below them, but it stopped early.

Maigret was mulling over these details as he lay dozing on his bed as he did every afternoon, while Madame Maigret sat reading by the window. Through his eyelids he could sense the golden half-darkness, the brighter stripes on the wall where the light filtered through the slats in the shutters.

His convoluted thoughts went round and round in his head, and suddenly he wondered, as if this question were paramount:

'Why that night?'

Why hadn't she been murdered the previous day, or the next, one month, two months earlier?'

The question seemed absurd, and yet, in his drowsy state, he saw it as being of the utmost importance.

For ten years, ten long years, she had lived alone in that quiet Vichy street. No one came to see her. She reportedly visited no one except, perhaps, during her brief monthly trips.

The neighbours saw her come in and go out. She could also be spotted sitting on a yellow chair in the park, drinking her glass of water or, in the evenings, in front of the bandstand listening to the concert.

Had he gone to speak to the shopkeepers himself, Maigret would have asked questions that would doubtless have surprised them.

'Did she sometimes engage in empty chatter . . . ? Would she sometimes bend down to stroke your dog . . . ? Did she talk to the housewives waiting in the queue and did she acknowledge the ones she ran into almost every day at the same time . . . ?'

And lastly:

'Did you ever see her laugh? . . . Or even smile . . . ?'

You had to go back more than fifteen years to find any personal contact with another human being: the man who came a couple of times a week to her apartment in Rue Notre-Dame-de-Lorette.

Can a person live for so many years without occasionally confiding in someone, without at least getting things off their chest out loud?

She had been strangled.

'But why that night?'

For the half-asleep Maigret, this became the key question and, when his wife informed him that it was three o'clock, he was still struggling to answer it.

'Did you sleep?'

'I dozed . . .'

'Are we both going out?'

'Of course we're both going out. Don't we do that every day? Why do you ask?'

'You might have arranged to meet Lecoeur.'

'I haven't arranged to meet anyone . . .'

And, to prove it, they went on a long walk, starting with the children's playground, then passing the boules games, the beach and then, after the Bellerive Bridge, continuing along the boulevard to the Yacht Club where they watched the water-skiers.

They went a lot further, towards the new apartment buildings which were twelve storeys high and rose white against the sky, creating a town on the fringes of the town.

On the opposite bank of the Allier, horses were galloping inside the white fences of the racecourse, and rows of heads and shoulders could be seen in the stands, as well as dark and light silhouettes on the grass.

'The hotel owner told me that more and more pensioners are coming to live in Vichy . . .'

He teased:

'Is that what you're preparing me for?'

'We have our house in Meung . . .'

They discovered quaint old streets. Each neighbourhood had its epoch, its own style. The houses were all different and you could guess the kind of person who had built them.

Maigret enjoyed stopping outside the little restaurants dotted around and reading the menus.

'Room for rent . . . Room with kitchen . . . Beautiful furnished room . . .'

That explained the restaurants, and also the tens of thousands of people milling around in the streets and along the promenades.

At five o'clock, they both sat down by the spring, their legs tired, and exchanged knowing smiles. Hadn't they overdone things a little? Were they not trying to prove to themselves that they were still young?

They recognized two faces among the crowd, the merry couple, and there was something different in the look that the man gave Maigret. Now, instead of walking past, he was making a beeline for Maigret with his hand outstretched.

What else could he do but shake it?

'Don't you recognize me?'

'I'm sure I have met you before, but I'm racking my brains . . .'

'Bébert, does that ring a bell?'

He had known a lot of Béberts, P'tit Louis and Grand Jules in the course of his career.

'The Métro . . .'

He turned to his wife as if seeking her confirmation and was merrier than ever.

'You arrested me for the first time on Boulevard des Capucines, on a day when there was a parade . . . I don't remember which head of state was strutting on horseback between the city guards . . . The second time was at the Métro exit at Bastille . . . You'd been following me for a while . . . It was some time ago . . . I was young . . . So were you, with all due respect . . .'

Maigret recalled the Métro arrest because, during the chase across Place de la Bastille, he'd lost his hat, a boater, as was fashionable at the time. Ha! That proved he'd already worn a straw hat.

'How long did you get?'

'Two years . . . That brought me to my senses . . . I went straight . . . First of all, I worked for a second-hand dealer where I patched up a load of junk, because I've always been good with my hands . . .'

A wink implied that had come in very useful when he made his living from pickpocketing.

'Then I met Madame . . .'

He said the word emphatically and also with a certain pride.

'No criminal record. She was never on the game. She'd barely arrived from Brittany and she was working in a dairy . . . With her, it was serious from the word go and we tied the knot officially . . . She even insisted we marry in her village church, and it was a proper white wedding . . .'

He loved life with every fibre of his being.

'I thought I recognized you . . . Every day I looked at you, but I wasn't sure . . . This morning, when I opened the newspaper and saw your photo . . .'

He pointed to the glass holders.

'It's not serious, I hope?'

'I'm in very good health . . .'

'So am I . . . All the doctors say so . . . They still sent me here because of the pains I get in my knees . . . Hydrotherapy, underwater massages, radiation therapy, the works . . . What about you?'

'Glasses of water . . .'

'Well, then it's nothing . . . But I don't want to keep you

or your dear lady . . . You were very decent with me, in the past . . . Those were the good old days, weren't they . . . ? Goodbye, inspector . . . Say goodbye, sweetie pie . . .'

As the couple walked off, Maigret was still smiling at the colourfulness and the fate of the former pickpocket. Then his wife saw his expression gradually cloud and his brow furrow. Finally, he gave a sigh of relief.

'I think I know why . . .'

'Why that woman was killed?'

'No . . . Why that particular day . . . Why not a month or a year ago . . .'

'What do you mean?'

'Since we've been here, we've met the same people two or three times a day, and their faces end up becoming familiar . . . It is only today, because of the photo in the newspaper, that that loony was certain he recognized me and came to talk to me . . .

'Now this is our first visit, our only one, most likely . . . If we were to return next year, we'd find a certain number of regulars . . .

'Someone is here in Vichy, like us, for the first time . . . He followed the routine, chose a doctor, was examined, had tests done, and was given his schedule, the names of the springs, the volume of centilitres to drink at such-and-such a time . . .

'He ran into Hélène Lange and thought he recognized her . . .

'Then he saw her a second time, and a third . . . Perhaps he wasn't far from her the other evening, when she was listening to the music . . .'

It all sounded quite simple to Madame Maigret and she was surprised that he was excited about a discovery that wasn't one.

Maigret quickly added, ironically:

'According to the publicity brochures, some two hundred thousand people take the waters here each year, over a six-month period. That means more than thirty thousand each month. Let's say a third of them are first-timers, like us, and that leaves some ten thousand suspects . . . No! Because we should rule out women and children . . . How many women and children, do you reckon?'

'More women than men . . . As for children . . .'

'Wait! . . . There are a number of people in invalid carriages . . . Others are on crutches or walk with sticks . . . Most of the old men would be incapable of strangling a woman who's still in her prime . . .'

She wondered whether he was being serious or whether he was joking.

'Let's say a thousand men physically capable of strangulation . . . And since we're talking about a tall, muscular individual, according to the eye-witness accounts of Madame Vireveau and the bar owner, that rules out the short and the puny men . . . That brings it down to five hundred . . .'

She was relieved to hear him laugh.

'Who are you laughing at?'

'The police. Our profession. Later on, I'm going to tell the good Lecoeur that he's only got five hundred suspects, unless we can eliminate any others, those who were at the theatre that night, for instance, and can prove it, the ones who were playing bridge or something else . . . and to think that this is often the way we arrest a culprit . . . ! Once, Scotland Yard questioned every resident in a town of two hundred thousand . . . It took months.'

'Did they find him?'

And Maigret replied:

'In a different town, by chance, one night when the fellow was drunk and talked too much.'

It would probably be too late to see Lecoeur that day, because he still had two glasses of water to drink, with an interval of half an hour in between. He tried to take an interest in the evening newspaper, which was full of articles about celebrities on holiday. It was quite curious. Even those who led a frenetic life had themselves photographed with their children or their grandchildren, claiming that they devoted all their time to them.

Later, when the breeze had become fresher, they turned the corner of Rue d'Auvergne. A van was parked outside Mademoiselle Lange's house.

As they drew near, they heard the sound of hammering.

'Shall I go back to the hotel?' murmured Madame Maigret.

'I'll be along in a minute . . .'

The lounge door was open and men in beige coats were hanging black drapes on the walls.

Lecoeur appeared.

'I thought you'd come . . . Step this way . . .'

He led Maigret into the bedroom, which was quieter.

'Is she being buried in Vichy?' asked Maigret. 'Is that what the sister decided?'

'Yes . . . She dropped in to see me before lunch . . .'

'With her gigolo?'

'No. By taxi . . .'

'When's the funeral?'

'In two days' time, to give the local people the opportunity to visit the chapel of rest . . .'

'Will there be an absolution?'

'Apparently not.'

'Wasn't the Lange family Catholic?'

'The old folk, yes . . . The girls were baptized and took their first communion . . . But since . . .'

'Unless she's divorced, for example . . . ?'

'First, there'd need to be proof that she was married . . .'

Lecoeur looked at Maigret while twirling the tips of his auburn moustache.

'You've never crossed paths with either of them in the past, I suppose?'

'Never . . .'

'But you spent a certain amount of time at La Rochelle . . .'

'I went there twice, let's say ten days in total . . . Why?'

'Because, this morning, I didn't find Francine Lange exactly the same . . . She was less chirpy . . . Her words didn't come out so directly . . . The entire time I had the impression that she had an ulterior motive, or that she wanted to tell me a secret . . .

'At one point, she said:

' "That was Inspector Maigret who was here yesterday, wasn't it?"

'I asked her if she'd met you before and she replied

that she'd recognized your photo in this morning's newspaper . . .'

'A few dozen people among the thousands I walk past each day had the same reaction . . . Earlier one of my former customers came up to shake my hand and was close to clapping me on the back . . .'

'I think it's more complicated,' said Lecoeur, as if he was following a train of thought that was still hazy.

'Do you think I might have had dealings with her at the time she was living in Paris?'

'It's not impossible, given the life she must have led there . . . No! What I'm thinking is less specific, subtler . . . As far as she's concerned, I'm an ordinary provincial police officer doing his job as best he can and asking the questions he has to ask . . . Once I've written down the replies, I move on to the next . . . Do you see what I mean . . . ? That explains why, when she walked in here, she was very relaxed and why, yesterday afternoon, she wasn't . . . She glanced over towards your corner a couple of times, but I could tell she hadn't recognized you . . .

'She's staying at the Hôtel de la Gare . . . As in most of the hotels here, the newspapers are taken up to the guests along with their breakfast . . . On seeing your photo, she wondered why you were present during our interview . . .'

'What do you conclude from that?'

'You're forgetting your reputation, the image the public has of you . . .'

He turned red, afraid his words might be misconstrued.

'And not only the public, in fact. In the profession we're the first—'

'Let's move on.'

'It's important . . . She said to herself that you weren't sitting there by chance . . . And, even if it was by chance, the fact that you are involved in the case—'

'Did she seem scared?'

'I wouldn't go that far. I found her different, on her guard. I only asked her inconsequential questions, but, each time, she took the trouble to think hard before replying . . .'

'She hadn't found the notary?'

'I thought of that as well, and I spoke to her about it . . . Her companion drew up a list of all the notaries in town and telephoned them . . . Apparently none of them had Hélène Lange as a client . . . Only one, who was a clerk ten years ago and who has since taken over his employer's practice, remembered having drawn up the deed of sale for this house . . .'

'Do you have his name?'

'Maître Rambaud . . .'

'Do you want to give him a call?'

'At this hour?'

'Provincial notaries generally live in the house where they have their practice . . .'

'What should I ask him?'

'Whether she paid by cheque or by bank transfer.'

'I'll have to ask the workmen to stop banging while I telephone . . .'

Meanwhile, Maigret wandered into the bathroom and the kitchen, not thinking about anything in particular.

'Well?'

'You guessed?'

'What?'

'She paid cash? It was the first time that had happened to our Rambaud, so he remembered it. She had a small suitcase stuffed with notes.'

'Have you questioned the ticket clerks at the station?'

'Heavens! I didn't think of that!'

'I'd be curious to know whether she went to the same or different places each month . . .'

'I hope to be able to tell you tomorrow . . . Enjoy your dinner . . . And have a pleasant evening!'

It was a concert evening at the bandstand and the Maigrets had walked enough to take a well-earned rest.

4.

He was ten minutes early, he didn't know why. Perhaps, that morning, there was less to read in *La Tribune*? Madame Maigret, who always used the bathroom after him, was still in there, and he said through the half-open door:

'I'm going down . . . Wait for me downstairs . . .'

There was a green seat on the pavement for the hotel's guests. The sky was still as blue. Since they'd been in Vichy, it hadn't rained once.

The owner was waiting for him at the foot of the stairs, as usual.

'So, what about this murderer?'

'It's not my case,' Maigret replied with a smile.

'Do you think those people from Clermont-Ferrand are up to the job? In a town like ours, it's not a good thing to have a strangler on the loose. Apparently several elderly women have already left . . .'

Maigret smiled vaguely as he made his way to Rue du Bourbonnais. From a distance he saw black drapes over the door with a large letter 'L' embroidered in silver. There was no police officer outside. Had there been one the previous day? He couldn't remember. He hadn't paid any attention. In short, this wasn't his case. He wasn't here in a professional capacity, he was just a visitor taking the waters.

He was about to press the bell when he noticed that the white door was open a fraction. He pushed it, saw a very young woman, barely sixteen, wiping a wet rag over the tiles in the hallway.

She wore a dress that was so short that when she bent over, it revealed her pink underwear. Her legs and thighs were pudgy and shapeless, as is often the case at that awkward age. They were like the legs of a cheap doll and were the same artificial colour.

When she turned around, he saw a moon face with expressionless eyes. She didn't ask who he was or what he was doing there.

'It's in there . . .' was all she said, pointing to the lounge door.

The room was dark, hung with black drapes, with the coffin resting on what must have been the dining-room table. The two candles weren't lit, but there was holy water in a glass bowl with a sprig of boxwood.

The dining-room door was open, so was that of the kitchen. In the dining room, the furniture and items from the lounge had been piled up. In the kitchen, young Dicelle was sitting in front of a cup of coffee, reading a comic album.

'Do you want some coffee too? I've made a full pot.'

. . . On the gas cooker of Hélène Lange, who would probably not have appreciated her kitchen being used in this way.

'Is Inspector Lecoeur not here?'

'He received an emergency call in Clermont-Ferrand late yesterday evening . . . There was a hold-up at the

Caisse d'Épargne, leaving one man dead, a passer-by who, on seeing the door ajar after closing time, pushed it open just as the thieves were coming out . . . One of them fired . . .'

'Nothing new here?'

'Not to my knowledge . . .'

'Did you take care of the railway station?'

'My colleague Trigaud's dealing with it . . . He's probably still there . . .'

'The young servant girl I've just seen has been questioned, I presume? What does she say?'

'From the look of her, it's already surprising that she can speak! She knows nothing. She was only hired for the season. Her job was to clean the lodgers' rooms. She didn't clean the ground floor because Mademoiselle Lange did her own housework . . .'

'She's never seen any visitors?'

'Only the man from the gas company and delivery boys. She started work at nine o'clock and finished at midday . . . The Maleskis upstairs are worried . . . They've paid up until the end of the month . . . They're wondering whether they'll be allowed to stay . . . It's not easy to find a room at the height of the season and they don't want to go to a hotel . . .'

'What did Lecoeur decide?'

'I think they're staying . . . In any case, they're up there . . . The other one, the fat woman, has just gone out to get herself pummelled by the masseurs . . .'

'Hasn't Francine Lange arrived?'

'I'm waiting for her . . . No one knows what's going to

happen . . . She insisted on having a chapel of rest set up, but I wonder whether anyone will come . . . My instructions are to stay here and keep a discreet eye on the visitors, if there are any . . .'

'Have a good day, all the same . . .' muttered Maigret, leaving the kitchen.

He automatically picked up a book bound in black cloth from a pedestal table which had been in the lounge and was now stashed with the rest of the furniture in the dining room. It was *Lucien Leuwen*. The yellowing pages had that particular musty smell of books from public libraries and bookshops that offer reading subscriptions.

A purple stamp gave the name and address of the bookshop owner.

He put the novel back on the table and, a moment later, he was walking calmly down the street. A window was flung open and a woman in curlers and a dressing gown called out to him:

'Tell me, inspector, is it true that we can visit?'

The expression surprised him and he stood there for a moment, baffled.

'I imagine so, since there's a chapel of rest and the door is half open . . .'

'Can you see her?'

'As far as I know, the coffin is sealed . . .'

She sighed:

'I prefer that . . . It's not so scary . . .'

He found Madame Maigret sitting on the green seat and she looked surprised to see him back so soon.

They started walking, like the other mornings. They

were only a few minutes behind schedule, a schedule which, in actual fact, they'd never drawn up but which they kept to as if it were of crucial importance.

'Are there many people?'

'No one. We're waiting . . .'

This time, they started out at the children's playground, which was still almost empty, and they walked around it in the shade of the trees. Some of these, like those bordering the Allier, were rare species, from America, India and Japan, and had both a Latin and a French name on a metal plaque. Many of them had been sent as gifts by forgotten heads of state, maharajas or minor oriental princes, in gratitude for a course of treatment at Vichy.

They barely paused by the boules players. Madame Maigret never asked her husband where he was going. He walked straight ahead, as if he had a goal, but, most of the time, if he chose one street rather than another, it was for a change, to encounter new images, new sounds.

Shortly before it was time for his glass of water, he went down Rue Georges-Clemenceau, as if he had some purchases to make, but he turned left into one of the passages, Passage du Théâtre, where outside a bookshop were second-hand books in boxes and other colourful books on revolving stands.

'Let's go in . . .' he said to his wife, who was hesitant.

The owner wore a long grey coat and was busy sorting out books. He appeared to recognize Maigret, but he waited.

'Do you have a few minutes?'

'At your service, Monsieur Maigret. I assume you wish to question me about Mademoiselle Lange?'

'She was one of your customers, wasn't she?'

'She came in at least once a week, more often twice, to change her books. She had a subscription that allowed her to borrow two books at a time . . .'

'Had you known her long?'

'I took over the shop six years ago. I'm not from here but from Paris, from Montparnasse. She already used to come when the previous owner—'

'Did you converse with her?'

'As you know, she wasn't very talkative . . .'

'She didn't ask you to recommend books for her to read?'

'She had her own ideas. Come and have a look over here . . .'

At the back of the bookshop was a room stacked from floor to ceiling with books bound in black cloth.

'She would often spend half an hour, even an hour, examining the books, reading a few lines of one and then another . . .'

'The last book she borrowed was Stendhal's *Lucien Leuwen*.'

'Stendhal was her most recent discovery . . . Before that she'd read all of Chateaubriand, Alfred de Vigny, Jules Sandeau, Benjamin Constant, Alfred de Musset, George Sand . . . Always the romantic novelists . . . Once, she took a Balzac, I don't remember which one, and brought it back the next day . . . I asked her if she'd disliked it and she answered something along the lines of:

' "It's too violent."

'Balzac, violent . . . !'

'No modern-day authors?'

'She never tried . . . On the other hand, she read and reread the letters of George Sand and Alfred de Musset . . .'

'Thank you . . .'

He'd almost reached the door when the bookshop owner called him back.

'I was forgetting a detail which you might find amusing. I was surprised to find the books annotated in pencil. Phrases and words were underlined. Sometimes there was a cross in the margin. I wondered which of my customers had this compulsion and I eventually found out it was her . . .'

'Did you mention it to her?'

'I had to . . . My assistant couldn't spend all day erasing those marks.'

'What was her reaction?'

'She looked offended and said:

' "I apologize . . . When I read, I forget the books don't belong to me . . ." '

The spa patients, the pale trunks of the plane trees and the patches of sunlight were all in position, as well as the thousands of yellow chairs.

She found Balzac too brutal . . . She probably meant too life-like . . . She confined herself to the first half of the nineteenth century, arrogantly ignoring Flaubert, Hugo, Zola and Maupassant . . . but all the same, on the first day, in a corner of the lounge, Maigret had spotted a pile of magazines.

He couldn't help trying to flesh out the picture he had built up of her. She only read romantic novels, but there was sometimes a note of real steeliness in her gaze.

'Have you seen Lecoeur?'

'No. He was called to Clermont-Ferrand because of a hold-up . . .'

'Do you think he'll find the killer?'

Maigret gave a start. It was his turn to be brought back down to earth. As a matter of fact, he wasn't thinking of the murder. He had almost forgotten that the owner of the house with green shutters had been strangled and that the most important thing was to catch her murderer.

He too was looking for someone. He even thought about it more often than he'd have liked, to the point where it was becoming an obsession.

What intrigued him was the man who, at one point, had found a place in this woman's solitary life.

There was no trace of him in Rue du Bourbonnais. There was no photograph of him, no letter or brief note.

Nothing! Nothing of anyone else either, apart from bills.

One had to go back to Paris, to Rue Notre-Dame-de-Lorette, twelve years earlier to find any mention of a rather hazy visitor who came once or twice a week and spent an hour in the apartment of the woman who was still young.

Even the sister, Francine, who lived in the same city at the time, claimed not to know anything.

Hélène Lange devoured books, watched television, did her shopping, her housework, went for walks in the shady park, like the people taking the waters, without speaking to a soul, and she listened to music by the bandstand staring straight ahead of her.

He found this disconcerting. In the course of his career, he had encountered individuals, men and women, fiercely attached to their freedom. He had met maniacs who'd withdrawn from the world to hide away in the most unlikely places, often the most squalid.

But these people always maintained some sort of connection to the outside world. For old women, it was a seat in a park, for example, where they'd meet another old woman, or the church, the confessional, the priest . . . Old men were regulars at a café where everyone knew them and casually greeted them . . .

In this case, for the first time, Maigret was up against solitude in its pure state.

A solitude that wasn't even aggressive. Mademoiselle Lange wasn't unpleasant towards her neighbours or the local shopkeepers. She didn't treat them with contempt and, despite her taste for certain colours and styles of dress, she did not put on airs.

Quite simply, she took no notice of others. She didn't need to. She took in lodgers because she had empty rooms and it gave her an income. But there was a dividing line between those rooms and the ground floor, and she'd hired a half-witted servant girl to clean the upstairs rooms.

'May I, detective chief inspector?'

A shadow in front of Maigret, a lanky form gripping the back of a chair. Maigret had seen the man at Rue du Bourbonnais. He was one of Lecoeur's colleagues, probably Trigaud. He sat down and Maigret asked:

'How did you know you'd find me here?'

'Dicelle told me—'

'And how did Dicelle . . . ?'

'There isn't a police officer in town who doesn't know you by sight, so that wherever you go—'

'Is there any news?'

'Last night, I spent an hour at the railway station, because it's not the same staff on duty as during the day . . . I went back there this morning . . . Then I telephoned Inspector Lecoeur, who's still in Clermont . . .'

'Won't he be coming today?'

'He doesn't know yet. In any case, he'll arrive early tomorrow for the funeral. I presume you'll be there too . . .'

'Have you seen Francine?'

'She dropped in to the funeral parlour . . . The transportation of the body will take place at nine o'clock . . . It was probably she who sent the flowers . . .'

'How many wreaths?'

'Just one . . .'

'Ascertain that it was her . . . I'm sorry! I'm forgetting that it's none of my business . . .'

'That's not what the chief thinks, because he told me to be sure to tell you what I discovered . . . I have the feeling there are some in the squad, including yours truly, who are about to go on a trip . . .'

'Did she go far?'

Trigaud pulled a wad of papers out of his pocket, and eventually found the one he was looking for.

'They don't remember all her journeys, of course, but

some names of cities struck them . . . For example, Strasbourg the month after a trip to Brest . . . They noticed
that the connections weren't always easy and she sometimes had to change trains two or three times . . .
Carcassonne . . . Dieppe . . . Lyon . . . That's not so far . . .
Actually Lyon was an exception . . . Most of the trips were
further . . . Nancy, Montélimar . . .'

'No small towns? No villages?'

'Only fairly large towns . . . True, she could have continued her journey by car because—'

'No tickets for Paris?'

'None . . .'

'Had it been going on for long?'

'The last clerk I questioned has been working at the
same ticket window for nine years.

'She was already a regular customer, he told me.

'The station staff knew her. They expected her. They
would sometimes bet on which town she'd choose next.'

'Were there specific dates?'

'No, that's the thing . . . Sometimes, they didn't see her
for six weeks, especially in summer, during the season,
probably because of her lodgers . . . Her trips didn't cor-
respond to the end of the month, or set intervals . . .'

'Did Lecoeur tell you what he plans to do?'

'He ordered a number of photographs . . . He'll begin
by sending men to the nearest towns . . . And today he'll
send photos to the local Police Judiciaire headquarters.'

'Do you know why Lecoeur wanted me to be informed?'

'He didn't say anything to me . . . He must think that
you have an idea . . . So do I, as a matter of fact . . .'

People always thought he was cleverer than he was and, if he protested, they were convinced it was a ploy.

'Are there many visitors at Rue du Bourbonnais?'

'According to Dicelle, it started at around ten a.m . . . A woman in an apron pushed open the door and poked her head round, then she took a few steps inside and found the chapel of rest . . . She took a rosary out of her apron pocket and her lips began to move . . . She made the sign of the cross with the holy water and then left . . .

'She was the one who triggered a stream of visitors . . . She informed the neighbours . . . Then the women came, alone or in pairs . . .'

'No men?'

'A few. The butcher, a carpenter who lives at the end of the street, people from the neighbourhood . . .'

Why would the murder not have been committed by someone local? They were busy looking everywhere, piecing together the life of the lady in lilac in Nice, in Paris, her trips to all four corners of France, but no one had thought of the neighbours, the thousands of people who lived in the France district.

Neither had Maigret.

'Is there anything I should be doing?'

It was not of his own accord that Trigaud spoke those words, which must have been suggested to him by that cunning Lecoeur. Since they had Maigret on hand, why not use him?

'I wonder whether the ticket clerks might remember some precise dates. Not many, two or three would be enough.'

'I already have one . . . The 11th of June . . . The fellow remembers because it was Reims, and his wife is from there and that day was her birthday . . .'

'If I were you, I'd go and check with the bank to see if there was a deposit on the 13th or the 14th . . .'

'I see what you mean . . . Blackmail, eh?'

'Or an allowance . . .'

'Why pay an allowance on different dates and at irregular intervals?'

'I'm wondering the same thing . . .'

Trigaud gave Maigret a funny look, convinced he was hiding something or that he was making fun of him.

'I'd rather deal with the hold-up,' he complained. 'With gangsters you generally know what to expect . . . I apologize for disturbing you . . . Good day, madame . . .'

He stood up, embarrassed, not knowing how to leave, and he had the sun in his eyes.

'It's too late for the bank . . . I'll go over there at two o'clock . . . Then, if necessary, I'll return to the station . . .'

Maigret too had once done that job, tramping around for hours, on burning or wet pavements, questioning people who were mistrustful and who he'd had to worm words out of one at a time.

'We must go for our glass of water . . .'

While Trigaud would probably quench his thirst with a large beer . . .

'See you at the spring, around eleven . . . I hope I'll be there . . .'

There was a hint of irritability in his voice. Madame Maigret had been worried he'd be bored in Vichy, doing nothing from morning till night with only her company. His smiling serenity of the first few days had only half reassured her, and she wondered how long that mood would last.

But now, for the past three days, he'd been genuinely annoyed each time he missed one of their walks.

Today was the funeral. He'd promised Lecoeur he'd attend. The sun was still shining and in the streets there was that same mixture of morning coolness and moisture.

Rue du Bourbonnais afforded an unusual sight. In addition to the residents who could be seen at their windows, resting on their elbows as if to watch a procession, curious onlookers lined the kerbs, forming a cluster close to the house of the dead woman.

The hearse had already arrived. Behind was parked a dark car, no doubt supplied by the undertakers, and then another which Maigret hadn't seen before.

Lecoeur came out to meet him.

'I had to abandon my gangsters,' he said. 'Hold-ups happen every day. The public's used to them and they aren't affected by them any more. Whereas a woman strangled in her own home in a quiet town like Vichy, without any apparent motive . . .'

Maigret recognized the auburn mop of the photographer from *La Tribune*. Two or three others were at work in the street and one of them snapped the two police chiefs crossing the road.

In short, there was nothing to see and the bystanders looked at one another as if wondering what they were doing there.

'Have you got men in the street?'

'Three . . . Dicelle doesn't appear to be here, but he can't be far away . . . He had the bright idea of asking the pork butcher's boy to come with him because he knows everybody . . . He'll be able to point out the people who aren't from this neighbourhood . . .'

There was nothing sad or awe-inspiring about the scene. Everyone was waiting, including Maigret.

'Are you going to the cemetery?' he asked Lecoeur.

'I'd like you to come with me, chief . . . I've brought my own car, thinking that a police car might be in bad taste . . .'

'Francine?'

'She arrived a few minutes ago with her gigolo . . . She's inside . . .'

'Where's their car?'

'The funeral directors, who know what's proper and what isn't on these occasions, probably explained to them that a red convertible was hardly any more appropriate for a funeral convoy than a police car . . . They'll be in the black saloon.'

'Did she speak to you?'

'She greeted me distractedly when she arrived . . . She seems on edge, worried . . . Before going inside the house, she scanned the throng as if she was searching for someone . . .'

'I still don't see your young Dicelle . . .'

'Because he's found a window somewhere for himself and his butcher's boy to watch the crowd.'

People came out of the house, and two more neighbours

94

went in, emerging almost immediately. Then the driver of the hearse clambered into his seat.

As if it were a signal, four men brought the coffin out, struggling to get it through the doorway, and slid it into the vehicle. One of them went back inside the house and returned with a wreath and a smaller bouquet.

'The bouquet is from the lodgers . . .'

Francine Lange waited on the doorstep, wearing a black dress that didn't suit her, which she must have bought the previous day in Rue Georges-Clemenceau. Her companion could be seen behind her in the dark hallway.

The hearse advanced a few metres. Francine and her lover got into the black car.

'Come on, chief . . .'

The people lining the street didn't move, and only the photographers ran down the middle of the road.

'Is that all?' asked Maigret turning around.

'There's no other family, no friends . . .'

'The lodgers?'

'Maleski has an appointment with his doctor at ten o'clock and fat Madame Vireveau has her massage . . .'

They drove past two or three streets which Maigret knew from having strolled down them on his wanderings. He filled his pipe, looked at the houses, and was surprised when the car came out in front of the station.

The cemetery wasn't far away – just across the railway line. It was deserted. The hearse drove as far as it was possible for motor vehicles to go.

So there were only four of them on a gravel path, apart from the undertakers. Lecoeur and Maigret instinctively moved closer to the couple. The boyfriend had put on a pair of shades.

'Will you be leaving Vichy soon?' Maigret asked the young woman.

He'd asked the question to make conversation, without attaching any importance to it, and he noticed that she was watching him intently, as if to find out whether there was an ulterior motive behind his words.

'I should probably stay on for two or three days to sort everything out . . .'

'What are you going to do about the lodgers?'

'I'll let them stay until the end of the month. There's no reason not to. I'll simply lock up the ground-floor rooms.'

'Are you planning to sell the house?'

She didn't have time to reply because one of the men in black was coming over to her. The coffin was carried on shafts along a narrower path to the edge of the cemetery, where there was an open grave.

A photographer – not the tall redhead, but another one – materialized from nowhere and took a few shots while the coffin was being lowered into the ground and as Francine Lange threw a shovelful of earth into the grave, on the instructions of the officiant.

A few metres away, beyond a low wall, was a waste ground where wrecked cars lay rusting and further away stood a few white houses.

The hearse drove off and so did the photographer. Lecoeur shot a look at Maigret, who didn't understand because he seemed lost in thought. What exactly was he thinking about? La Rochelle, which he was fond of; Rue

Notre-Dame-de-Lorette, back in his early days when he was secretary to the superintendent of the ninth arrondissement; the boules players too . . .

Francine was walking towards them, a balled handkerchief in her hand. It hadn't been used to dry her tears. She hadn't cried. She had been no more emotional than the undertakers or the grave-digger. There had been nothing moving about that funeral, which had been as unromantic as could be.

If she was fiddling with her handkerchief, it was to keep her composure.

'I don't know what usually happens . . . Normally, after a funeral, there's a meal, isn't there . . . ? But I'm sure you have no wish to have lunch with us . . .'

'My work . . .' mumbled Lecoeur.

'Can I at least invite you for a drink?'

Maigret was surprised at the change in her. Here too, in the deserted cemetery, from which even the photographer had disappeared, she kept looking about her as if some danger lurked.

'I'm sure we'll meet on another occasion,' replied Lecoeur diplomatically.

'You still haven't found anything?'

It wasn't him she looked at as she asked the question but Maigret, as if she expected something of him.

'The investigation continues . . .'

Maigret filled his pipe with little movements of his index finger, trying to understand. This woman had certainly had a few knocks and was capable of facing up to life without batting an eyelid. It wasn't the death of her

97

sister that was affecting her, because, on the first day, she'd been full of life and energy.

'In that case, gentlemen . . . I don't know what else to say . . . Goodbye, then . . . And thank you for coming.'

Had she stayed a minute longer, Maigret would perhaps have asked whether anyone had threatened her. She walked off, teetering on her high heels, and as soon as she closed her hotel room door, she would tear off that black dress bought for the occasion.

'What do you think?' Maigret said to his colleague from Clermont.

'Did you notice as well . . . ? I'd like to interview her between four walls, but I'll have to think of a plausible reason to summon her. Today, it would be inappropriate . . . She seems to be afraid . . .'

'I had that feeling too . . .'

'Do you think she's received threats? What would you do in my shoes?'

'What do you mean?'

'We don't know why her sister was strangled . . . It could be a family drama after all . . . We know almost nothing about these people . . . It could be some business that both women were mixed up in . . . Didn't she tell you that she'd be staying another couple of days in Vichy . . . ? I don't have many men available, but the hold-up can wait . . . We always catch the professionals in the end . . .'

Now they were in the car, driving towards the cemetery exit.

'I'll have her watched as discreetly as possible, although,

in a hotel, that's almost impossible . . . Where shall I drop you off?'

'Somewhere near the park . . .'

'Of course you're here to take the waters . . . I don't know why I can't get that into my head . . .'

At first, he thought his wife hadn't arrived yet, because he couldn't see her on her chair. They were so used to meeting at the same place every day that he was surprised to find her on a different chair, in the shade of another tree.

He observed her for a moment without her spotting him. She didn't look impatient. In a pastel dress, her hands in her lap, she was watching the people walking past. A faint smile of contentment lit up her face.

'You're here!' she exclaimed.

Then, immediately:

'Our chairs are taken . . . I listened to them talking and I believe they're Dutch . . . I hope they're only passing through and that we won't find them in our seats every day . . . I didn't think it would be over so quickly . . .'

'The cemetery isn't far.'

'Were there a lot of people?'

'In the street . . . Afterwards, there were only four of us . . .'

'Did she bring her lover? Come and have a glass . . .'

They had to queue for a while, then Maigret bought the Paris newspapers, which barely mentioned the Vichy strangler. Only one, the previous day, had published a headline saying: 'The Vichy Strangler'. And, below it was a photo of Maigret.

He was curious to find out the result of the inquiries

carried out in some of the towns the lady in lilac visited on irregular dates.

Even so, his thoughts were vague. He read, his mind elsewhere, and over the top of his newspaper he could see the outlines of the promenaders. Soon they had to shift their chairs back because they were now in the sun.

That was what was good about the spot that had been taken over by the Dutch. It was in a place the sun didn't reach at the times they were in the park.

'Don't you want a newspaper?'

'No . . . The merry couple have just gone past and they gave you a big wave . . .'

They had already melted into the crowd.

'Did the sister cry?'

'No.'

He was still thinking about her. If he'd been in charge of the investigation, he too would have liked to question her in the calm atmosphere of his office.

He thought about her again several times during the rest of the morning. They walked back to the Hôtel de la Bérézina, went upstairs to freshen up, and sat down to lunch. As always, partially drunk bottles of wine were on each table except for theirs, next to glass vases containing two or three flowers.

'There's escalope Milanese or calf's liver *à la bourgeoise* . . .'

'Escalope,' he sighed. 'They'll serve mine without the sauce in any case. I'm just passing through, but Rian will still be here next year and the following years. He's the one who's important . . .'

'Don't you feel better than in Paris?'

'Only because I'm not in Paris. Besides, I never felt really bad. Lethargy, dizziness, I imagine it happens to everyone . . .'

'But you trust Pardon, don't you?'

'I have to . . .'

They had eaten all the pasta they'd been given for the hors d'oeuvre and starter and had just been served the escalopes when Maigret was told there was a phone call for him.

The telephone was in a small sitting room that looked out on to the street.

'Hello! I hope I'm not disturbing you . . . ? You're already having lunch . . . ?'

He recognized Lecoeur's voice and muttered:

'If you can call it that!'

'There's been a development . . . I'd sent one of my men to watch the Hôtel de la Gare . . . Before taking up his position he had the bright idea of asking for Francine Lange's room number . . . The receptionist looked surprised and told him she'd left . . .'

'When?'

'Barely half an hour after saying goodbye to us . . . Apparently the pair of them came back and before going up to their room, the man asked them to prepare the bill . . . They must have packed their bags at top speed because, ten minutes later, they telephoned to have their bags brought down . . .

'They crammed everything into the red car and drove off into the traffic . . .'

Maigret said nothing, neither did Lecoeur, and there was a fairly long silence.

'What do you make of that, chief . . . ?'

'She's scared . . .'

'Obviously, but she was already scared this morning, it was noticeable . . . Even so, she told us she was planning to stay in Vichy for another two or three days . . .'

'Maybe so you wouldn't detain her . . . ?'

'What right would I have had to detain her, unless I'd had something on her?'

'You know the law, but she doesn't.'

'We'll find out this evening or tomorrow morning whether she's gone home to La Rochelle . . .'

'It's most likely . . .'

'I think so too, but all the same I'm furious . . . I intended to see her again and have a long chat with her . . . It's true that I might learn more . . . Are you free at two o'clock?'

That was when Maigret took his nap and he replied reluctantly:

'I don't have anything particular to do, naturally.'

'While I was out of the office this morning, someone telephoned the local police station and asked to speak to me . . . I'm here at the moment . . . In the end I accepted the office they offered to lend me . . . It was a girl who gave her name as Madeleine Dubois . . . And guess what her job is . . . ?'

Maigret said nothing.

'She's the night telephonist at the Hôtel de la Gare. My Vichy colleague told her that I'd probably be in my office, in Avenue Victoria, by around two p.m . . . He asked her whether she could tell him what she was calling about, but she preferred to see me in person . . . I'm expecting her shortly . . .'

'I'll be there . . .'

He didn't have a nap but discovered the charming white turreted residence surrounded by gardens that was the Vichy police headquarters. A police officer led him down a corridor on the first floor where an office almost empty of furniture had been put at Lecoeur's disposal.

'It's five to two . . .' said Lecoeur. 'I hope she's not going to change her mind . . . That reminds me, I'd better find a third chair . . .'

He could be heard opening doors in the corridor until he found what he was looking for.

On the dot of two o'clock the duty officer knocked on the door and announced:

'Madame Dubois . . .'

She came into the room, a petite, lively woman with dark hair and a very mobile gaze that darted from one man to the other.

'Who should I speak to?'

Lecoeur introduced himself but didn't mention Maigret, who sat down in a corner.

'I don't know if what I have to tell you is of any use to you . . . At the time, I didn't attach any importance to it . . . The hotel's full . . . I had a lot of work, up till one o'clock in the morning, then, as usual, I went to sleep . . . It's about one of our guests, Madame Lange . . .'

'I presume you mean Mademoiselle Francine Lange?'

'I thought she was married. I know that her sister's dead

103

and that she was buried this morning . . . Last night, at about half past eight, someone asked to be put through to her . . .'

'A man?'

'A man, yes, with a very strange voice . . . I'm almost certain he suffers from asthma, because I had an uncle who had it and who spoke just like that—'

'He didn't give his name?'

'No.'

'He didn't ask for the room number?'

'No . . . I rang but no one answered . . . So I told him that the person he wished to speak to was not in her room . . . He called again at around nine o'clock and there was still no answer from room 406 . . .'

'Mademoiselle Lange and her companion had only one room for the two of them?'

'Yes . . . The man called back a third time at eleven o'clock and, this time, Mademoiselle Lange answered . . . I put him through . . .'

She looked embarrassed, glanced over at Maigret as if to gauge the effect her next words would have on him. She too must have recognized him.

'Did you listen in . . . ?' asked Lecoeur kindly.

'I'm sorry . . . I don't normally . . . We have a reputation for eavesdropping, but if people knew how uninteresting it is, they'd think differently . . . Perhaps it's because of the sister's murder . . . Or because of the man's strange voice . . .

' "Who's calling?" she asked.

' "Am I speaking to Mademoiselle Francine Lange?"

' "Yes . . ."

' "Are you alone in the room?"

'She hesitated. But I was almost positive her companion was with her.

' "Yes . . . and what business is that of yours?"

' "I have a confidential message for you . . . Listen carefully . . . If we're cut off, I'll call you back in half an hour . . ."

'He was wheezing, sometimes making a sort of whistling sound, like my uncle.

' "I'm listening . . . You still haven't told me who you are . . ."

' "That doesn't matter . . . It is essential that you remain in Vichy for a few days . . . It is in your interest . . . I'll contact you, I'm not sure when yet . . . Our conversation could earn you a very large sum of money . . . Do you understand . . . ?"

'He stopped talking and hung up. After a few minutes, room 406 rang.

' "Mademoiselle Lange here . . . I have just received a telephone call . . . Can you tell me whether it came from Vichy or elsewhere?"

' "From Vichy."

' "Thank you."

'There . . . At first, I thought it was none of my business. Then, this morning, I was unable to go to sleep and I telephoned here to ask who was in charge of the investigation . . .'

She fiddled anxiously with her handbag, her gaze flitting between the two men.

'Do you think it's important?'

'You haven't been back to the hotel?'

'I'm not on duty again until eight o'clock this evening . . .'

'Mademoiselle Lange has left.'

'Didn't she go to her sister's funeral?'

'She left Vichy almost immediately afterwards.'

'Oh!'

Then, after a silence:

'You think that man wanted to lure her into a trap, don't you? He wouldn't happen to be the strangler, would he?'

She turned pale at the idea of having had the murderer of the lady in lilac on the end of the line.

Maigret did not regret missing his nap.

5.

Once the telephonist had left, the two men stayed where they were, Maigret puffing on his pipe, Lecoeur smoking a cigarette that came close to singeing his moustache. The smoke hung in wisps above their heads. In the courtyard, a dozen or so officers could be heard doing gymnastics.

There was a prolonged silence. Both were seasoned veterans who knew the ins and outs of the job. They'd had dealings with all sorts of criminals, all sorts of witnesses.

'It was obviously the killer who telephoned . . .' sighed Lecoeur at length.

Maigret didn't reply immediately. They didn't react in the same way. Without mentioning the word 'methods', one which neither of them liked, they had different approaches to a problem.

Now, since the lady in lilac had been strangled, Maigret had not thought a great deal about the murderer. This was not deliberate. He was somehow haunted by the woman, whom he kept seeing in his mind's eye, sitting on her yellow chair in front of the bandstand, with her long face and gentle smile, which was sometimes belied by the steeliness of her gaze.

That image had been fleshed out a little when he'd visited the house in Rue du Bourbonnais, learned about her time in Nice, her life in Paris, or at least the little that was known, and even the books she read.

The strangler was only a shape, a tall, muscular man whom Madame Vireveau claimed to have seen on the corner of the street, walking very fast, and a bar owner had noticed without being able to make out his features.

Imperceptibly, Maigret was starting to think about him.

'I wonder how he found out that Francine Lange had booked into the Hôtel de la Gare . . .'

The newspapers that had reported on the arrival of the victim's sister had not given the address where she was staying.

Maigret advanced cautiously, hesitantly.

'Why would he not quite simply have telephoned different hotels and asked to speak to Mademoiselle Lange . . .'

He imagined him in front of a telephone directory. The list of hotels must be very long. Had he proceeded in alphabetical order?

'You could perhaps call a hotel whose name begins with A or with B . . .'

With an amused look in his eye, Lecoeur picked up the receiver.

'Would you get me the Hôtel d'Angleterre? . . . No. Not the management, or reception. I'd like to speak to the telephonist . . . Hello! Are you the telephone operator at the Hôtel d'Angleterre? . . . This is the Police Judiciaire . . . Has someone asked to be put through to a certain Mademoiselle Lange? . . . No, not the victim . . . Her sister, Francine Lange . . . That's right . . . Ask your colleague . . .'

He informed Maigret:

'There are two of them on the switchboard . . . The hotel has five or six hundred rooms . . . Hello, yes . . . Yesterday morning? . . . Pass me your colleague, would you? . . . Hello! Was it you who took the call? . . . Nothing struck you? . . . A croaky voice, you say? . . . As if the man . . . Yes . . . I understand . . . Thank you . . .'

And to Maigret:

'Yesterday morning, at around ten . . . A croaky voice, or rather that of a man who has trouble breathing . . .'

Someone who was taking the waters, as Maigret had thought from the very first day, and who had run into Hélène Lange by chance . . . He'd have followed her to find out where she lived . . .

The telephone rang. It was the inspector who'd been sent to Lyon. He'd discovered no trace of the victim in the town's hotels, but a post-office clerk remembered her. She'd come twice, both times to collect a fat padded envelope. The first time, the envelope had been waiting for a week. The second time, it had just arrived.

'Do you have the dates?'

Lost in thought, still puffing avidly on his pipe, Maigret watched his colleague at work.

'Hello! Crédit Lyonnais? . . . Have you got that list of deposits I requested? . . . No . . . I'll have someone collect it later . . . Can you tell me if a payment was received immediately after the 13th of January last year and another the 22nd of February this year? . . . I'll hold on, yes . . .'

It didn't take long.

'A deposit of eight thousand francs on the 15th of

January . . . Another of five thousand on the 23rd of February this year . . .'

'The average deposit is five thousand francs, is that correct?'

'Nearly all are . . . With a few rare exceptions . . . I have the statement in front of me . . . I see that, five years ago, the sum of twenty-five thousand francs was credited to the account . . . It is the only deposit of that size . . .'

'Always in cash?'

'Always.'

'What is the balance on the account at present?'

'Four hundred and fifty-two thousand, six hundred and fifty . . .'

Lecoeur repeated the figure to Maigret.

'She was rich . . .' he muttered, 'and yet she rented out furnished rooms during the season . . .'

He was surprised to hear Maigret reply:

'He's very rich . . .'

'It's true . . . It appears that this money all comes from the same source . . . A man who can pay five thousand francs a month, occasionally larger sums . . .'

But that man was not aware that Hélène Lange was the owner of a little white house with pale green shutters in Vichy's France neighbourhood. Each time he sent money, it was to a different address.

Was the money not sent on a fixed date and did Mademoiselle Lange deliberately not pick it up until a few days later so as to be certain that her chosen post office wasn't being watched?

A wealthy man, or in any case, very comfortably off . . .

When he'd spoken to the sister on the phone, he hadn't made a precise arrangement . . . He'd asked her to stay in Vichy a few days longer, and to wait for his call . . . Why?

'He must be married . . . He's here with his wife and perhaps his children . . . He's not free when he wants . . .'

Now Lecoeur was intrigued to watch Maigret's brain at work. Was it really his brain, though? He was now trying to get under the man's skin.

'Rue du Bourbonnais, he didn't find what he was looking for . . . and Hélène Lange didn't talk . . . If she'd talked, she probably wouldn't have died . . . He wanted to frighten her to get the information he needed out of her . . .'

'So, despite his wife, he was free that evening . . .'

Maigret fell silent, pondering this objection.

'What was on at the theatre on Monday?'

Lecoeur picked up the telephone to inquire.

'*Tosca* . . . It was a sell-out . . .'

This wasn't rigorous reasoning, true. It wasn't even reasoning. Maigret tried to imagine a man, a fairly important figure, probably staying at one of the best hotels in Vichy. He had his wife, his friends . . .

The previous day or the day before that, he'd run into Hélène Lange and followed her to find out where she lived.

That evening, *Tosca* was being performed at the Grand Casino theatre. Aren't women fonder of Italian opera than men?

'*Why don't you go without me? . . . I'm tired from my treatment . . . I'll take the opportunity to have an early night . . .*'

What information did he want from Hélène Lange and why did she obstinately refuse to talk?

Had he gone into the house before her, forcing an easy lock, and searched her apartment before she arrived home?

Or had he only turned up once she was back home, and had he already killed her when he ransacked the place?

'Why that little smile, chief?'

'Because I'm thinking of a stupid detail . . . Before the Hôtel de la Gare, the murderer must, if he went in alphabetical order, have made thirty or so phone calls . . . Does that not suggest something to you . . . ?'

He filled a fresh pipe.

'The entire police force is looking for him . . . His wife is probably staying with him in a hotel room . . . However, he has to repeat numerous times a surname that is the same as that of the victim . . .

'In hotels, all calls go through the switchboard . . . Furthermore, there's his wife to contend with . . .

'It's risky to telephone from a café, or a bar, where there's the possibility of being overheard . . .

'If I were you, Lecoeur, I'd have a certain number of men watching the public call-boxes . . .'

'But he did get hold of Francine Lange!'

'He's going to call her back . . .'

'She's not in Vichy any more . . .'

'He doesn't know that . . .'

In Paris, like most husbands, Maigret saw his wife three times a day: when he woke up, at midday and in the evening. Although he sometimes didn't go home for lunch.

So during the rest of the day he could have got up to anything without her knowing.

But in Vichy? They were together almost twenty-four hours a day, and he wasn't the only one in this situation.

'He can't even linger too long in a call-box . . .' Maigret sighed.

He probably went out to buy cigarettes or get a breath of fresh air while his wife was getting dressed. One or two telephone calls . . . If she was taking the waters as well, and if she was having hydrotherapy, that gave him a little more time to himself . . .

He imagined this man taking advantage of every opportunity, creating them, like a kid lying to his mother.

A portly man of a certain age, wealthy, with an important job, in Vichy to try to find a cure for his asthma . . .

'Does it not surprise you that the sister left?'

Francine Lange liked money. Goodness knows what she'd got up to when she lived in Paris to come by it. Now she owned a thriving business. She was going to inherit her sister's fortune.

But was she the sort of woman to thumb her nose at a large sum?

Was it the police she feared? It seemed unlikely. Unless she'd decided to flee for good, to go abroad.

No! She'd returned to La Rochelle, where the police could question her just as well as in Vichy. For the time being, she was still on the road, her boyfriend at the wheel, while youths turned their heads to stare enviously after the red convertible.

'She'll arrive around mid-afternoon, because they must be driving fast . . .'

'Have the newspapers mentioned that she lives in La Rochelle?'

'No . . . They only reported her arrival . . .'

'She was already afraid this morning, at the funeral parlour and at the cemetery . . .'

'I wonder why it was you she was looking at covertly . . .'

'I think I understand . . .'

Maigret smiled, not without embarrassment.

'The press has given me a reputation as a sort of confessor . . . She must have been tempted to confide in me, to ask me for advice . . . Then she said to herself that it was too big a thing . . .'

Lecoeur frowned.

'I don't see . . .'

'The man tried to get a piece of information out of Hélène Lange and this information was important enough to make him lose all control . . . It's rare for someone to strangle a person in cold blood . . . He came to Rue du Bourbonnais unarmed . . . He didn't intend to kill . . . But he left empty-handed . . .'

Thinking of the strangling, Maigret added:

'So to speak . . .'

'He presumes the sister has the same piece of information?'

'It's certain . . . Otherwise, he wouldn't have gone to so much trouble and he wouldn't have taken so many risks to find out where she was staying . . . He wouldn't have telephoned her and wouldn't have hinted to her about the payment of a large sum . . .'

'What about her? Does she know what he wants from her?'

'It's possible . . .' muttered Maigret checking the time on his watch.

'It's likely, isn't it . . . ? As is proved by the fact that she was scared enough to leave without telling us anything . . .'

'I have to go and meet my wife . . .'

He nearly added:

'Like the other fellow!'

Like that portly man with broad shoulders who had to make up childish excuses to go and telephone from a call-box.

Who knows? In the course of their daily strolls, the Maigrets had perhaps walked past that couple several times. It was possible that they'd sat next to them when drinking their glass of water, that their chairs—

'Don't forget the phone booths . . .'

'I need as many men as you have in Paris . . .'

'I never have enough . . . When are you going to call La Rochelle?'

'At around six o'clock, before I leave for Clermont-Ferrand, where I have an appointment with the examining magistrate . . . He's waiting for me at his home . . . This case is troubling him because he's closely connected with the Compagnie de Vichy, which doesn't appreciate this kind of publicity . . . If you want to be present . . .'

Madame Maigret was waiting for him on a bench. Never in their lives had the Maigrets sat on so many park benches and chairs. He was late, but she didn't reprimand him, contenting herself to observe that he seemed to be in a different mood from earlier.

She knew that expression, half frowning, half pensive.

'Where are we going?'

'For a walk . . .'

Like the other days. Like the other couple. The wife wouldn't suspect anything. She went for strolls with her husband unaware that he quaked at the sight of every police uniform.

He was a murderer. He couldn't run away without coming under suspicion. Like the Maigrets, he had to carry on with his daily routine.

Was he staying in one of the two or three luxury hotels? It was none of Maigret's business, but if he were Lecoeur . . .

'Lecoeur is an excellent police officer . . .' he muttered.

Which meant, deep down:

He's bound to think of it. There aren't so many guests, in those hotels, for . . .

But he wished he could go and sniff around himself.

'Don't forget your appointment with Rian . . .'

'Is it today?'

'Tomorrow, at four o'clock.'

Once again he'd have to get undressed, allow himself to be prodded and poked, clamber on to the weighing machine and listen to the fair-haired young doctor earnestly discussing the amount of water he was to drink from now on. Was he going to send him to a different spring?

He thought of Janvier, who'd moved into his office because Lucas was on holiday too. He'd chosen the mountains, somewhere near Chamonix.

A string of small sailing boats were slowly tacking into the wind. Couples on pedalos drifted by and there were miniature golf courses every fifty metres along the wall bordering the Allier.

Maigret caught himself turning around each time they passed a portly man of a certain age.

For him, Hélène Lange's killer had stopped being a shadowy image. He was beginning to take shape, to acquire a personality.

He was in the town, somewhere on one of the walks the Maigrets took with such regularity. His movements were similar to theirs, and he saw the same sights, the sailing boats, the pedalos, the yellow chairs in the park and the crowd strolling by at a monotonous pace.

Rightly or wrongly, Maigret saw him with a wife at his side, a fairly plump woman too, complaining her feet hurt.

What did they talk about as they walked? What did all those couples among whom the Maigrets found themselves say to each other?

He had killed Hélène Lange . . . He was wanted. One word, one gesture, one slip-up and he'd be arrested.

His entire life destroyed. His name on the front page of the newspapers. His friends flabbergasted, his fortune and that of his family jeopardized.

A police cell instead of a comfortable apartment . . .

The transformation could happen within a few minutes, a few seconds. A stranger was perhaps going to tap him on the shoulder and, when he looked around, he would find himself face to face with a police badge.

'Are you Monsieur . . . ?'

Monsieur who? It didn't matter. The shock, his wife's outrage.

'It must be a mistake, inspector . . . I know him well . . . He's my husband . . . Everyone will tell you . . . Speak up for yourself, Jean!'

Jean, or Pierre, or Gaston . . .

Maigret kept covertly looking around him.

'But he's still trying . . .'

'He's still trying to what?'

'Trying to find out the truth . . .'

'What are you talking about?'

'You know who I'm talking about . . . He telephoned Francine Lange . . . He wants to talk to her . . .'

'Won't he get caught?'

'If she'd told Lecoeur in time, they'd have set up a trap . . . It's still possible . . . He's not familiar with her voice . . . Lecoeur is bound to have thought of that . . . He just needs to put a woman of around her age in room 406 . . . When the man calls—'

Maigret stopped in his tracks and growled, his fists clenched, as if enraged:

'What the hell can he be looking for to take such a huge risk?'

A man's voice replied:

'Hello! Who do you wish to speak to?'

'I'd like to speak to Mademoiselle Francine Lange . . .'

'Who's calling?'

'Chief Superintendent Lecoeur . . .'

'One moment, please . . .'

Maigret was sitting facing Lecoeur in the bare office and was holding the extra listening device to his ear.

'Hello! . . . Could you call back tomorrow morning?'

'No . . .'

'In half an hour?'

'In half an hour, I'll be on the road . . .'

'We've only just got here. Francine . . . I mean Mademoiselle Lange, is in her bath—'

'Ask her from me to get out of it . . .'

Lecoeur winked at his Paris colleague. Once again, Lucien Romanel's voice could be heard.

'She'll be with you in a moment . . . She's just drying herself . . .'

'I get the impression that you didn't drive very fast . . .'

'We broke down We lost nearly an hour trying to find a spare part . . . Here she is . . .'

'Hello . . .'

Her voice sounded more distant than that of her boyfriend.

'Mademoiselle Lange? This morning, you told me that you'd be staying in Vichy for another two or three days . . .'

'That was my intention . . . I changed my mind . . .'

'May I ask why?'

'I could answer that I changed my mind, and that's that. I have a right to, don't I?'

'And I have a right to request a court order and force you to talk . . .'

'What difference does it make whether I'm in Vichy or La Rochelle?'

'For me, a very big one . . . Now, I repeat my question: what made you change your mind?'

'I was scared . . .'

'Of what?'

'You know very well . . . I was already afraid this morning, but I told myself he wouldn't dare . . .'

'Could you be clearer, please? Afraid of whom?'

'Of the man who strangled my sister . . . I thought that if he went for her, he's capable of going for me . . .'

'For what reason?'

'It's hard to say . . .'

'Do you know him?'

'No . . .'

'You don't have the slightest idea who it could be?'

'No . . .'

'And yet, at midday, having just told me you'd be extending your stay in Vichy, you left the hotel in a great hurry . . .'

'I was scared . . .'

'You are lying . . . Or, to be more specific, you had a particular reason to be scared . . .'

'I told you . . . He killed my sister . . . He could just as easily—'

'For what reason?'

'I don't know . . .'

'And you don't know why your sister was killed either?'

'If I knew, I'd have told you . . .'

'In that case, why haven't you told me about the telephone call?'

He imagined her, in her bathrobe, her hair damp, in the apartment where the suitcases had just been opened. Did her telephone have a second earpiece? Otherwise Romanel must be standing in front of her darting her questioning looks.

'What telephone call?'

'The one you received yesterday evening at your hotel . . .'

'I don't see what you—'

'Do I need to remind you what the caller said? Did he not advise you to stay in Vichy for another two or three days? Did he not tell you that he'd be back in touch with you and that you could receive a very large sum of money?'

'I barely listened . . .'

'Why?'

'Because I thought it was a joke . . . Is that not your impression?'

'No.'

A very sharp 'no' followed by a menacing silence. On the other end of the line, she was unnerved and was struggling to find something to say.

'Well, I'm not from the police . . . I'm telling you I thought it was a practical joke . . .'

'Do people often play this sort of practical joke on you?'

'Not this sort . . .'

'Was it not that telephone conversation that frightened you enough to make you leave Vichy as quickly as possible?'

'Because you don't believe me . . .'

'I'll believe you when you're telling the truth . . .'

'It scared me . . .'

'What?'

'Knowing that the man was still in town . . . All women must be frightened at the idea of a strangler roaming the streets . . .'

'Although the hotels haven't suddenly emptied . . . Have you ever heard that voice before?'

'I don't think so . . .'

'A very distinctive voice . . .'

'I didn't notice . . . I was too surprised . . .'

'Earlier, you mentioned a bad joke . . .'

'I'm tired . . . The day before yesterday I was still on holiday in the Balearics . . . I've barely slept since . . .'

'That's no reason to lie . . .'

'I'm not used to being questioned . . . Especially over the telephone, after being dragged out of my bath . . .'

'If you prefer, in one hour, you'll receive an official visit from my colleague in La Rochelle and everything you say will be duly taken down . . .'

'I'm doing my best to answer you . . .'

Maigret's eyes were laughing. Lecoeur was doing a good job. That was not how he would have gone about it himself, but the result would have been the same.

'You knew yesterday that the police were looking for your sister's murderer . . . You were not unaware that the slightest clue could be valuable . . .'

'I suppose so . . .'

'And there is every chance that your invisible caller could be the murderer . . . That occurred to you . . . You were even certain of it, because you were frightened . . . Now you are a woman who's not faint-hearted—'

'I might have thought it, but I wasn't certain . . .'

'In your shoes, anyone else would have rung us to inform us . . . Why did you not do so?'

'You're forgetting that I'd just lost my sister, who was my only relative, and that her funeral took place today . . .'

'And you weren't upset in the slightest . . .'

'How do you know?'

'Answer my question . . .'

'You might have detained me . . .'

'It's not urgent business that's calling you back to La Rochelle, because you were supposed to be staying in the Balearics a few days longer . . .'

'I found the atmosphere oppressive . . . The idea that this man—'

'Was it not rather the idea that, following that phone call, we might ask you certain questions?'

'You might have used me as bait . . . When he called me back to arrange a meeting, you'd have sent me there and . . .'

'And . . . ?'

'Nothing . . . I was scared . . .'

'Why was your sister strangled?'

'How am I supposed to know?'

'Someone tracked her down after a number of years, followed her, broke into her home—'

'I thought she'd caught him red-handed burgling her . . .'

'You are not so naive . . . He had a question he wanted to ask her, a crucial question . . .'

'What?'

'That's what I'm trying to find out . . . Your sister had come into an inheritance, Mademoiselle Lange . . .'

'From whom?'

'That's what I'm asking you.'

'We both inherited from my mother . . . She wasn't rich . . . A haberdashery in Marsilly and a few thousand francs in savings . . .'

'Was her lover wealthy?'

'What lover?'

'The one in Paris who used to go and see her once or twice a week in her apartment in Rue Notre-Dame-de-Lorette . . .'

'I don't know anything about it . . .'

'You never met him?'

'No . . .'

'Don't hang up, mademoiselle . . . This is likely to continue for some time . . . Hello? . . .'

'I'm still here . . .'

'Your sister was a shorthand typist . . . You were a manicurist—'

'I became a beautician . . .'

'Fine . . . Two young women from Marsilly whose parents had no money . . . You both go to Paris . . . You don't arrive together, but, for several years, the two of you see each other . . .'

'What's so unusual about that?'

'You claim you know nothing of your sister's doings . . . You can't even tell me where she worked . . .'

'First of all, there was the age difference between us . . . And then, we never got along well, even when we were little . . .'

'I haven't finished . . . It happens that soon, we find you, still young, owner of a hair salon in La Rochelle which must have cost you a lot of money . . .'

'I paid part of the purchase price through annuities . . .'

'It is possible that, later on, we may need more details regarding that matter . . . Meanwhile, your sister vanishes from sight, so to speak . . . First of all, she spends five years in Nice . . . Did you go and visit her?'

'No.'

'Did you have her address?'

'She sent me three or four postcards . . .'

'In five years?'

'We had nothing to say to each other . . .'

'What about when she moved to Vichy?'

'She didn't tell me . . .'

'She didn't write to say that she was now living in this town and had bought a house here?'

'I found out through friends . . .'

'What friends?'

'I don't remember . . . People who'd met her in Vichy . . .'

'And who'd spoken to her?'

'Possibly . . . You're getting me confused . . .'

Lecoeur, pleased with himself, winked again at Maigret, whose pipe had gone out and who was engaged in a complicated manoeuvre to fill another one without letting go of the earpiece.

'Did you go to the Crédit Lyonnais?'

'What Crédit Lyonnais?'

'The one in Vichy . . .'

'No . . .'

'You weren't curious to find out how much you were going to inherit?'

'My notary here is dealing with the estate . . . I don't understand anything about these things . . .'

'Even though you're a businesswoman . . . Do you have any idea how much your sister had in the bank?'

There was another silence.

'I'm listening . . .'

'I can't answer you . . .'

'Why not?'

'Because I don't know . . .'

'Would you be surprised to learn that it is close to five hundred thousand francs?'

'That's a lot . . .'

She said that calmly.

'It's a lot for a little typist who left Marsilly one fine day and only worked for around ten years in Paris . . .'

'She didn't confide in me . . .'

'Think before you answer, because we have ways of checking whether or not you are speaking the truth . . . When you moved to La Rochelle, was it not your sister who made the initial payments?'

Another silence. And silence makes much more of an impression over the telephone than when you have a person in front of you. There is a total cut-off.

'Do you need to think?'

'She lent me a little money . . .'

'How much?'

'I'll have to ask my notary . . .'

'At that time, was your sister not living in Nice?'

'It's possible . . . Yes . . .'

'So you were in touch with her . . . Not only through an exchange of postcards . . . It is likely you went to see her to tell her about your project . . .'

'I must have gone there . . .'

'You told me the opposite a moment ago . . .'

'Your questions are getting me all muddled up . . .'

'They are perfectly straightforward, but your answers are less so . . .'

'Have you finished?'

'Not yet . . . and I would advise you more strongly than ever not to hang up, which would force me to take some rather unpleasant steps . . . This time, I want a clear answer, yes or no . . . Whose name is on the deed of sale of the business, yours or your sister's? In other words, was your sister the real owner?'

'No.'

'Are you?'

'No.'

'Who is?'

'Both of us.'

'So you were partners and you are trying to have me believe that you had no contact with your sister . . .'

'That's family business and it's nothing to do with anyone else . . .'

'It is when there's a murder . . .'

'It has nothing to do with—'

'Are you certain?'

'I don't suppose . . .'

'You suppose it so little that you left Vichy in a panic . . .'

'Do you have any more questions?'

Maigret nodded, grabbed a pencil from the desk and scribbled a few words on a notepad.

'Just a moment . . . Don't hang up . . .'

'Is this going to take much longer?'

'Now . . . You had a child, didn't you?'

'I told you about it.'

'You gave birth in Paris?'

'No.'

'Why not?'

Maigret's note read simply: *Where did she give birth? Where was the child registered?*

'I didn't want anyone to know . . .'

Lecoeur probed further, perhaps because of the presence of his illustrious Paris colleague.

'Where did you go?'

'To Burgundy.'

'Where exactly?'

'Mesnil-le-Mont . . .'

'Is that a village?'

'More of a hamlet . . .'

'Is there a doctor there?'

'There wasn't in those days.'

'And you chose to give birth in a hamlet where there was no doctor?'

'How do you think our mothers managed?'

'Was it you who chose that place? Had you already been there?'

'No. I looked at a road map . . .'

'Did you go there alone?'

'I wonder how you interrogate criminals if this is how you torment people who've done nothing and who, on the contrary—'

'I asked you if you went there alone . . .'

'No.'

'That's better. You see, it's easier to tell the truth than to be evasive. Who was with you?'

'My sister.'

'You do mean your sister Hélène?'

'I don't have any others.'

'This was the time when you both lived in Paris and you only met by chance . . . You didn't know where she worked . . . She could just as well have been a kept woman . . .'

'That was none of my business . . .'

'You didn't like each other . . . You had as little to do with each other as possible, but she suddenly gave up her job to go with you to a godforsaken hamlet in Burgundy . . .'

Francine Lange had nothing to say.

'How long did you stay there?'

'A month.'

'At a hotel?'

'At the inn . . .'

'Did a midwife assist you?'

'I'm not sure she was a midwife, but she helped all the local pregnant women . . .'

'What is her name?'

'She was over sixty-five at the time . . . She must be dead . . .'

'You don't recall her name?'

'Madame Radèche . . .'

'Did you register the child at the town hall?'

'Of course . . .'

'Yourself?'

'I was confined to bed . . . My sister went with the owner of the inn, who acted as witness . . .'

'Did you see the register of births, later?'

'Why would I have gone to see it?'

'Do you have a copy of the birth certificate?'

'It was so long ago . . .'

'Where did you go after that?'

'Listen, I can't take any more . . . If you absolutely insist on questioning me for hours, come and see me here.'

Undeterred, Lecoeur asked:

'Where did you take the child?'

'To Saint-André . . . Saint-André-du-Lavion, in the Vosges.'

'By car?'

'I didn't have a car in those days.'

'Your sister neither?'

'She's never driven.'

'Did she go with you?'

'Yes! Yes! Yes! And now, make whatever you like of it . . . I'm sick and tired of this, do you hear? Sick! Sick! Sick!'

Upon which, she hung up.

6.

'What are you thinking about?'

The question asked by all couples, all those who live side by side for years observing each other, who, coming against an unreadable expression or look, can't help timidly inquiring:

'What are you thinking about?'

Admittedly, Madame Maigret only asked the question when she sensed her husband was relaxed, as if there was a zone she knew she was not allowed to enter.

After the long telephone call to La Rochelle, there had been the calm of dinner, in the restful white hotel dining room with its potted plants and its bottles of wine and flowers on the tables.

Nobody appeared to take any notice of the Maigrets, even though they were still the object of a discreet curiosity, both admiring and affectionate.

Now, it was their evening stroll. Rumbles of thunder could be heard somewhere in the sky, and suddenly the still air was whipped up by gusts of wind.

As if automatically, they'd walked down Rue du Bourbonnais, where there was a light at one of the first-floor windows, in plump Madame Vireveau's room. The Maleskis were out, either on a walk or at the cinema.

The ground floor was dark and silent. The furniture was back in place. Hélène Lange had been erased.

One day, probably, the contents of the house would be piled up on the pavement and a jaunty auctioneer would sell off everything that had been the trappings of a life.

Had Francine taken the photographs? It was unlikely. It was also unlikely that she'd send for them. They would be auctioned off along with everything else.

They were walking in the direction of the park, where walks almost inevitably ended up, when Madame Maigret had asked her question.

'I was thinking that Lecoeur is an excellent investigator,' replied her husband.

The questions the chief inspector from Clermont-Ferrand had fired off, without allowing Francine the time to collect herself, were calculated to fluster her. He'd got the very most out of the facts in his possession and obtained tangible results that would provide a basis for the next stages of the investigation.

Why was Maigret not entirely satisfied? He would have taken a different approach, probably. Two men, even if they apply the same method, do things differently.

But this wasn't about method. Deep down, Maigret envied his colleague's brilliance, his assurance, his self-confidence.

For Maigret, the lady in lilac was not simply the victim of a murder, nor a person who had led a particular type of existence. He was beginning to know her and he was trying, almost unwittingly, to learn more about her.

It was the story of the two sisters that was uppermost

in his mind as he walked, whereas a carefree Lecoeur had cheerfully gone off to his appointment with the examining magistrate.

What could the latter really know about the case, cloistered in his chambers where everything that had been alive was summed up in the formal language of official reports?

Two sisters, in a village on the Atlantic coast, in a shop near the church. Maigret knew that village, where people worked both the land and the sea. Four or five large-scale operators owned the oyster farms and mussel beds.

He pictured the women, young and old, including little girls, setting out in the early hours, sometimes in the dark, depending on the tides. Wearing rubber boots, they were dressed in thick woollens and cast-off men's jackets.

On the beach, they gathered the oysters from the exposed beds while the men collected the mussels clustered in ropes spiralling around posts.

Most of the girls didn't have their school certificate and the boys had barely gone further; in any case, that's how it was when the Lange sisters lived in the village.

Hélène was an exception. She had gone to school in the town and had gained enough of an education to land an office job.

Setting off on her bicycle in the morning and coming home in the evening, she was a young lady.

And, later, her sister must have found a way to get by too, mustn't she?

'They're both in Paris . . . They aren't seen around the village any more . . . They look down on us . . .'

Their former friends continued to scrabble around in

the oyster beds in the morning and to collect mussels. They had married and raised children who now played in Place de l'Église.

Hélène Lange had achieved her ambitions by dint of a steely determination. Very young, she had rejected the life she'd been destined for and carved out a different path, choosing a personal world illustrated in her eyes by a few romantic novelists.

Balzac was too harsh for her, too close to Marsilly, to the family shop and the mussel beds where the cold froze your hands.

Francine had escaped too, in her own way. At fifteen, a taxi-driver had deflowered her and she didn't see why she shouldn't be liberal with her attractive, curvaceous body, why she shouldn't use her provocative smile to entice men.

Hadn't they both, ultimately, been successful?

The owner of the house in Vichy had a large sum of money in the bank and the younger sister, back home, flaunted her wealth by owning the town's best beauty salon.

Did Lecoeur not feel the need to live with them, to understand them? He established the facts, made deductions and, consequently, felt no qualms.

A man was mixed up in these two lives, a man whose face no one knew but who was somewhere there in Vichy, in his hotel room, in an avenue in the park, or in a room of the Grand Casino.

That man had killed. He was hunted. He could not be unaware that the police, with the huge resources at their disposal, were imperceptibly closing in on him and would narrow the field until the moment when an indifferent hand would come down on his shoulder.

He too had a life behind him. He had been a child, a young man, in love, probably married, because the stranger who visited Rue Notre-Dame-de-Lorette in Paris one or two evenings a week only stayed there for an hour.

Hélène disappeared and resurfaced, alone, in Nice, where she seems to have voluntarily lost herself in the anonymous crowd.

Before that, she made a detour via a little village in Burgundy, staying for a month at an inn with her sister, who had given birth.

That man too, Maigret needed to know him. He was tall and strong. His asthma, for which he was probably receiving treatment, gave him a distinctive voice.

He had killed for nothing. He had gone to Rue du Bourbonnais not to kill, but to ask a question.

Hélène Lange had held her tongue. Even when he'd grabbed her throat to scare her, she'd refused to speak, and she had paid for her silence with her life.

He could have given up. Caution demanded it. Any move on his part became risky. The police machine had been set in motion.

Did he already know she had a sister, Francine Lange? She claimed he didn't, and that was possibly true.

He had learned of her existence and that she had just arrived in Vichy from the press. He got it into his head to contact her, employing all his patience and cunning to find out the name of the hotel where she was staying.

Whereas Hélène had refused to talk, would the younger sister resist the lure of a large sum of money?

The man was rich, important. Otherwise, how would he have transferred more than five hundred thousand francs over the past few years?

Five hundred thousand francs in exchange for nothing. He received nothing. He didn't even know the whereabouts of the woman to whom he sent the money in cash to the different poste-restante addresses indicated by her.

Otherwise, would Hélène Lange not have been dead sooner?

'Stay in Vichy for another two or three days . . .'

He tried his last chance, at the risk of getting caught. He was going to telephone. He was perhaps doing so. It all depended on when he could give his wife the slip for a moment.

Now one of Lecoeur's men was watching the public telephone booths.

Had Maigret been wrong in thinking that he wouldn't call from a café or bar, or from his hotel room?

He and his wife walked past one of those call-boxes. Through the glass, they could see a very young girl talking excitedly.

'Do you think he'll get caught?'

'Very soon, yes.'

Because this man wanted something too desperately. Who knows whether he hadn't been living for years with this obsession, since, each month, he had been sending money constantly hoping for this coincidence that had taken fifteen years to occur?

He was perhaps an excellent businessman who never lost his composure in his day-to-day life.

Fifteen years dwelling on one fixation . . .

He had squeezed hard, without intending to kill. Unless . . .

Maigret stopped in his tracks in the middle of an avenue, and his wife automatically stopped, glancing at him briefly.

. . . Unless he had found himself in the face of something so monstrous, so unexpected, so unacceptable . . .

'I wonder how Lecoeur will go about it,' he muttered.

'To do what?'

'To get him to confess . . .'

'First of all they have to find him and arrest him . . .'

'He'll allow himself to be arrested . . .'

It would be a relief for him not to have to seek, to cheat, to—

'He isn't armed, is he . . . ?'

Because of his wife's question, Maigret envisaged a new prospect. Instead of surrendering, the man might decide to end it once and for all . . .

Had Lecoeur advised his officers to tread warily? Maigret couldn't interfere. In this case, he was merely a passive onlooker, staying discreetly in the background.

Even if the murderer allowed himself to be arrested, why would he talk? It would make no difference to what he'd done, to the jury's decision. For them, he was a strangler, and stranglers did not inspire lenience, even less sympathy, whatever their story.

'Admit that you'd like to have handled . . .'

In Vichy she permitted herself to make observations that she would never have made in Paris. Because they were on holiday? Because they were spending every hour of the day together and a closer relationship was developing between them?

She could almost hear him thinking.

'I wonder . . . No . . . I don't think so . . .'

Why was he worrying? He was here to cleanse his system, as Doctor Rian called it. As a matter of fact, his appointment with the doctor was tomorrow and, for half an hour, he would simply be a patient concerned about his liver, his stomach, his spleen, his blood pressure and his dizzy spells.

How old was Lecoeur? Barely five years younger than him. In five years, Lecoeur too would start thinking about retirement and asking himself how he'd spend his days.

They walked past the two most luxurious hotels in Vichy, behind the Casino. Limousines stood idle by the kerb. A man in a dinner-jacket was sitting in a garden chair beside the revolving doors, getting a breath of fresh air.

A crystal chandelier illuminated the lobby with its oriental carpets and marble columns, and a concierge in a tasselled uniform was answering the questions of an elderly lady in an evening gown.

It was perhaps in this hotel that the man was staying, or the one next door, or again the Pavillon Sévigné, near the Bellerive Bridge. A young bellboy, his gaze indifferent, waited by the lift.

Lecoeur had attacked the weakest point, in other words, Francine Lange, and, caught off-guard, she'd had a lot to say.

He would most likely arrange to question her again. Would he learn anything new from her? Had she not disclosed everything she knew?

'One moment . . . I need to buy some tobacco . . .'

He walked into a noisy café, where most of the customers were watching the television mounted on the wall above their heads. The air reeked of wine and beer. The bald owner was continuously filling glasses which a girl in a black dress and white apron carried over to the tables.

He automatically glanced over at the telephone booth at the back of the room, next to the toilet. It had a glazed door. The booth was empty.

'Three packets of shag . . .'

They weren't far from the Hôtel de la Bérézina now and, as they approached, they spotted young Dicelle on the steps.

'May I have a quick word with you, chief?'

Madame Maigret went straight inside and took her key from the board.

'Why don't we go for a walk?'

The streets were empty. Footsteps echoed from a distance.

'Did Lecoeur advise you to come and see me?'

'Yes. I got him on the phone. He was at home, in Clermont, with his wife and children . . .'

'How many children does he have?'

'Three . . . The eldest is eighteen and might become a champion swimmer—'

'What's going on?'

'About ten of us are watching the telephone booths . . . The chief inspector doesn't have enough men to have one for each booth, so we chose the ones in the centre, especially those that aren't too far from the main hotels . . .'

'Have you arrested someone?'

'Not yet . . . I'm waiting for Inspector Lecoeur, who must be on his way . . . It all went wrong and it's my fault . . . I was staking out a booth on Boulevard Kennedy . . . It was easy to hide, thanks to the trees . . .'

'Did a man go in to make a phone call?'

'Yes . . . A tall, corpulent man answering to the description we'd been given . . . He seemed wary . . . He looked around him but couldn't see me . . .

'He began by dialling a number . . . Did I poke my head out too far? . . . It's possible . . . It's also possible that he suddenly changed his mind . . . After dialling three digits, he stopped dead and came out of the booth . . .'

'Did you arrest him?'

'My instructions were not to arrest him under any circumstances but to follow him. I was surprised to see him, less than twenty metres away, join a woman who was waiting for him in the shadows . . .'

'What kind of woman?'

'A very elegant woman of around fifty . . .'

'Did they appear to be making an arrangement?'

'No. She took his arm and they headed towards the Hôtel des Ambassadeurs . . .'

The hotel whose lobby and crystal chandelier Maigret had gazed at an hour earlier.

'And then?'

'Nothing. The man went over to the concierge who gave him his key and wished him goodnight . . .'

'Did you get a close look at him?'

'Fairly close . . . In my opinion, he's older than his wife . . . He must be getting on for sixty . . . They went into the lift and I didn't see them again . . .'

'Was he in a dinner-jacket?'

'No . . . He was wearing a very well-cut dark suit . . . He has silver hair combed back, a rosy complexion and, I think, a little white moustache . . .'

'Did you question the concierge?'

'Of course. The couple is in room 105, on the first floor, a large bedroom and a lounge . . . It's their first year in Vichy, but they know the owner, who also has a hotel in La Baule . . . The man is Louis Pélardeau, a manufacturer who lives in Paris, Boulevard Suchet . . .'

'Is he taking the waters?'

'Yes . . . I asked whether he had a particular way of speaking and the concierge confirmed that he's asthmatic . . . Doctor Rian is treating both of them . . .'

'Is Madame Pélardeau taking the waters too?'

'Yes . . . They don't appear to have any children . . . They've met up with friends from Paris at the hotel and they share a table in the dining room . . . Sometimes they go to the theatre together . . .'

'Is someone watching the hotel?'

'I've put a reserve officer on guard duty until a colleague arrives at the scene, which he probably has by now . . . The officer, who could have told me to get lost, was very cooperative . . .'

Dicelle was worked up.

'What do you think? . . . It's him, isn't it?'

Maigret didn't answer right away but took the time to rekindle his pipe. They weren't a hundred metres from the house of the lady in lilac.

'I think it's him . . .' he sighed.

The young inspector looked at him in amazement, because he could have sworn that Maigret said those words reluctantly.

'I have to wait for my boss in front of the hotel . . . He should be here within the next twenty minutes . . .'

'Did he ask for me to be present?'

'He said you'd most likely come with me . . .'

'I'll have to tell my wife first . . .'

At the Grand Casino theatre, the interval had discharged a huge crowd into the street, and many of the audience, especially women in flimsy dresses or gowns with plunging necklines, glanced anxiously up at the sky streaked with flashes of lightning.

Low clouds scudded past, but above all, coming from the west, there was a dark, ominous-looking, almost solid mass.

Outside the Hôtel des Ambassadeurs, Maigret and Dicelle waited in silence while, behind his varnished wood desk, against a background of pigeonholes and dangling keys, the concierge watched them.

Lecoeur arrived just as huge drops of cold rain began to fall and the bell signalling the end of the interval was ringing. He had to carry out a few tricky manoeuvres to park his car, and at last he was making his way towards them, his brow furrowed.

'Is he in his room?' he asked.

Dicelle hastily replied:

'Room 105, on the first floor. His windows overlook the street . . .'

'Is his wife there too?'

'Yes. They came back together . . .'

A shape emerged from the shadows and a police officer whom Maigret didn't know came and asked quietly:

'Do I carry on watching?'

'Yes . . .'

Lecoeur lit a cigarette and sheltered in the doorway.

'I'm not authorized to carry out arrests between sunset and sunrise except in cases of *flagrante delicto* . . .'

He recited the article from the Code of Criminal Procedure with a certain amount of irony, adding pensively:

'I don't even have enough charges against him to obtain an arrest warrant . . .'

He seemed to be asking Maigret to come to his rescue, but the latter didn't react.

'I don't like letting him stew all night . . . He must know he's been identified . . . Something happened that stopped him making his phone call . . . The presence of his wife a few metres from the phone box baffles me . . .'

He added reproachfully:

'You're not saying anything, chief?'

'I have nothing to say . . .'

'What would you do in my shoes?'

'I wouldn't wait either . . . I'd avoid going upstairs,

143

where they're probably getting undressed . . . It would be more discreet to send him a note . . .'

'Saying what, for instance?'

'That there is someone in the lobby who has a personal message for him . . .'

'Do you think he'll come down?'

'I'd bet on it . . .'

'Will you wait for us here, Dicelle? There's no need for us to go into the hotel in force . . .'

Lecoeur went over to the concierge while Maigret remained standing in the middle of the lobby, vaguely surveying the vast, almost empty lounge. All the chandeliers were lit and, far away, in another world it seemed, four elderly people, two men and two women, were playing bridge with slow gestures. The distance created an unreal impression, like a scene shot in slow motion.

The bellboy hurried over to the lift, an envelope in his hand. Lecoeur said wearily:

'We'll see what happens . . .'

Then, as if struck by the solemn atmosphere, he removed his hat. Maigret too had his straw hat in his hand. Outside, the storm raged and the rain beat down. Several people were sheltering in the doorway, only their backs visible.

The bellboy wasn't gone long, and he came over to say:

'Monsieur Pélardeau is on his way down now . . .'

They couldn't help turning towards the lift. Maigret noticed a certain excitement in his colleague, who was smoothing his moustache between his thumb and first finger.

A bell from above. The lift rose and stopped for a moment, then soon reappeared.

A man with a rosy complexion and silver hair, dressed in dark clothes, stepped out. He scanned the lobby and walked towards the two men with a questioning look.

Lecoeur had his police badge in the hollow of his palm, and he flashed it discreetly.

'I should like to interview you, Monsieur Pélardeau.'

'Now?'

It was indeed the croaky voice that had been described. The man didn't panic. He had definitely recognized Maigret and seemed surprised to see him playing a silent part.

'Now, yes. My car is outside. I'll drive you to my office . . .'

His face became less rosy. Pélardeau was around sixty, but held himself very erect, maintaining a great deal of dignity in his bearing and facial expressions.

'I presume there's no point refusing?'

'None, other than to complicate matters . . .'

A glance over at the concierge, and then at the lounge where the four far-off silhouettes could still be seen. A glance too at the driving rain.

'It is unnecessary for me to go upstairs and fetch a hat or a raincoat, isn't it?'

Maigret met Lecoeur's gaze and rolled his eyes upwards. It was pointless and cruel to leave Pélardeau's unsuspecting wife alone up there. It was going to be a long night, and there was little chance that her husband would be coming back to reassure her.

Lecoeur muttered:

'You may send a note up to Madame Pélardeau . . . Unless she knows all about it . . .'

'No . . . What should I write?'

'I don't know . . . That you're going to be detained longer than you expected?'

The man went over to the desk.

'Have you got a piece of paper, Marcel?'

He was sad rather than overwhelmed or afraid. With the blue ballpoint pen lying on the desk he wrote a few words and refused the envelope that the concierge held out to him.

'Wait a few minutes before you take it up . . .'

'Very well, Monsieur Pélardeau . . .'

The concierge wanted to add something, cast around for something to say, but, at a loss, he remained silent.

'This way . . .'

Lecoeur gave instructions in a low voice to Dicelle, who was already soaked to the skin and opened the rear car door.

'After you . . .'

The manufacturer bent down and got into the car first.

'You too, chief . . .'

Maigret understood that his colleague didn't want to leave their prisoner alone in the back. A moment later, they were driving through the streets where some people were running while others sheltered under the trees. Some were even on the bandstand, where the musicians usually sat.

The car turned into the courtyard of the police headquarters in Avenue Victoria, and Lecoeur merely needed to say a few words to the officer on guard duty. Only some of the lamps were lit in the corridors and it felt like a long walk for Maigret.

'Come in . . . It's not comfortable, but I'd rather not take you to Clermont-Ferrand right away . . .'

He removed his hat and wondered whether to slip off his jacket whose shoulders, like those of the other two men, were wet. In comparison with the sudden coolness outside, it was very warm in the room where the air was stale.

'Please sit down . . .'

Maigret went over to his corner and slowly filled his pipe without taking his eyes off the manufacturer's face. Pélardeau had sat down on a chair and waited, outwardly calm.

It was a dramatic, almost heartbreaking calm, Maigret sensed. Not a muscle of the man's face moved. His eyes went from one police officer to the other, and he was probably trying to understand why Maigret was taking a back seat.

Lecoeur took his time, busying himself with a notepad and pencil, and muttered, as if to himself:

'Your answers to my questions will not be recorded because this is not an official interrogation . . .'

The man inclined his head in consent.

'Your name is Louis Pélardeau and you are a manufacturer. You reside in Paris, Boulevard Suchet.'

'That is correct.'

'You are married, I assume?'

'Yes.'

'Do you have children?'

There was a hesitation, and he said with a strange bitterness:

'No.'

'Are you here for a treatment?'

'Yes.'

'Is this the first time you have come to Vichy?'

'I have driven through the town . . .'

'Never to meet a specific person?'

'No.'

Lecoeur inserted a cigarette in his cigarette holder, lit it and remained silent for a good while.

'You are not unaware, I presume, of the reason why I have brought you here?'

Pélardeau thought, his face still inscrutable, but Maigret had already understood. His composure, his expressionlessness, was not so much self-control but the effect of an extreme emotion.

He was in a state of shock, and goodness knows how the images around him appeared to him, how Lecoeur's voice sounded to his ears.

'I would rather not answer . . .'

'You followed me without objecting . . .'

'Yes . . .'

'Were you expecting this to happen?'

He turned towards Maigret as if to ask him for help, then he repeated wearily:

'I would rather not answer . . .'

Lecoeur scribbled a word on his notepad and tried a different line of attack.

'Here in Vichy you had the surprise of running into a person whom you hadn't seen for fifteen years . . .'

His eyes were slightly moist, but there was no sign of

tears. It was perhaps the effect of the bright light. This room, at the end of a corridor, was used so seldom that it barely had any furniture and the lighting was reduced to a bare bulb dangling from a wire.

'This evening, when you went out with your wife, did you plan to stop to make a telephone call?'

He hesitated, then nodded.

'So your wife doesn't know?'

'About the phone call I had to make?'

'If you like.'

'No.'

'She is unaware of some of your doings?'

'Absolutely.'

'Even so, you went into a public phone booth . . .'

'She decided to come with me at the last minute . . . I didn't have the patience to wait for a new opportunity . . . I told her I'd left the key to our suite in the door and that I needed to phone the concierge . . .'

'Why did you not finish dialling the number?'

'I could sense I was being watched . . .'

'You didn't see anything?'

'Something moved behind a tree . . . At the same time, I thought that making the phone call was pointless . . .'

'Why?'

He didn't reply. His hands rested flat on his knees, slightly pudgy hands, white and manicured.

'If you wish to smoke . . .'

'I don't smoke . . .'

'Does it bother you if we do?'

'My wife smokes a lot . . . Too much . . .'

'You suspected that it wasn't Francine Lange who would be picking up the phone?'

Once again, he did not reply, but nor did he deny it.

'You called her yesterday evening . . . You said you would ring back to arrange to meet her . . . I have every reason to assume that, by this evening, you had decided on the time and the place for this meeting . . .'

'I apologize for not being more cooperative . . .'

He had to get his breath back and his words were interspersed with a slight wheezing from his throat.

'It is not unwillingness on my part, believe me . . .'

'Are you waiting to be assisted by a lawyer?'

His right hand made a vague sweeping gesture, as if to dismiss that idea.

'But you will have to hire one . . .'

'I will, because the law demands it . . .'

'Do you understand, Monsieur Pélardeau, that from now on, you will be deprived of your freedom?'

Lecoeur had been tactful enough not to utter the word 'prisoner' and Maigret was grateful to him.

The man inspired respect in both of them, especially in that cramped office with neutral-coloured walls. Sitting on a spindle chair, he looked larger than life and he maintained an astonishing calm, an unexpected dignity.

Between them they had interviewed hundreds of suspects and it took a lot to affect them. This evening, they were impressed.

'I could postpone this conversation until tomorrow, but that would be pointless, wouldn't it?'

The man seemed to think that that was the chief inspector's business, and not his.

'Incidentally, what branch of industry are you in?'

'Wire production . . .'

They were broaching a subject he could talk about and he provided some details, as if not to say no to everything, or routinely remain silent.

'I inherited from my father a fairly modest wire works, near Le Havre . . . I expanded it, and built others in Rouen, and then in Strasbourg . . .'

'So you're the head of a large company?'

'Yes.'

He sounded apologetic.

'Your offices are in Paris?'

'The headquarters. We have more modern offices in Rouen and Strasbourg, but I was keen to keep the old head office on Boulevard Voltaire . . .'

For him, that was the past. Within a few minutes, that evening, while a bellboy in gold-braided livery holding a note was going up in the lift, an entire part of his life had ceased to exist.

He knew it and that was perhaps why he let himself talk about it.

'How long have you been married?'

'Thirty years . . .'

'You once employed a certain Hélène Lange?'

'I'd rather not answer.'

That was his response each time they touched on the sensitive point.

'Do you realize, Monsieur Pélardeau, that you are not making my job any easier?'

'I'm sorry.'

'If you intend to deny the facts that I am going to have to accuse you of, I'd rather know right away . . .'

'I don't know what you are going to say . . .'

'Do you claim you are innocent?'

'In one way, no . . .'

Lecoeur and Maigret exchanged glances, because he had just said that terrible word simply, naturally, without a muscle of his face moving.

Maigret recalled the shady areas in the park, the greenery which, in some places, took on surreal hues under the lamplight, the musicians in their colourful uniforms.

Above all, he pictured the long, thin face of Hélène Lange, who was still, for him and his wife, just the lady in lilac.

'Did you know Mademoiselle Lange?'

He remained stock still, holding his breath, as if he was suffocating. He was having an asthma attack. His face turned very red. He pulled a handkerchief from his pocket, opened his mouth and began to cough uncontrollably, his body bent double.

Maigret was glad he wasn't in his colleague's shoes. For once, he was leaving the unpleasant task to someone else.

'I . . .'

'Take your time, please . . .'

His eyes misty, he desperately tried to stop the coughing fit, which lasted several minutes.

When he sat up, still crimson, he began by mopping his face.

'I'm sorry . . .'

His voice was barely audible.

'It happens several times a day . . . Doctor Rian says that the waters will do me good . . .'

He was suddenly struck by the irony of those words.

'I mean: would have done me good . . .'

They had the same doctor, he and Maigret. They had undressed in the same gloss-painted room, lain on the same bed covered in a white sheet . . .

'You asked me . . . ?'

'Whether you knew Hélène Lange . . .'

'It would be pointless to deny it . . .'

'Did you hate her?'

If Maigret had been able to, he would have gestured to his colleague that he was taking the wrong tack.

And indeed, the man looked at Lecoeur with an astonishment that was not feigned and, for a moment, this sixty-year-old figure displayed an almost childlike candour.

'Why?' he murmured. 'Why would I have hated her?'

He turned to Maigret as if seeking an ally.

'Did you love her?'

They were presented with an unexpected transformation. He frowned, trying to understand. The last two questions had surprised him, as if everything was being called into question.

'I really don't see . . .' he stammered.

Then, once again, he looked from one to the other, letting his gaze dwell on Maigret's face.

They sensed there was a misunderstanding somewhere.

'You used to visit her in her apartment in Rue Notre-Dame-de-Lorette . . .'

'Yes . . .'

He seemed to be implying: 'but what does that matter?'

'I presume it was you who paid the rent?'

He nodded discreetly.

'Was she your secretary?'

'One of my employees . . .'

'Your relationship lasted several years . . .'

Visibly, the misunderstanding persisted.

'I would go and see her once or twice a week . . .'

'Did your wife know?'

'No, of course not . . .'

'She found out at one point?'

'Never . . .'

'What about now?'

Poor Pélardeau gave the impression of a man who was constantly banging up against the same wall.

'Not now either . . . It has nothing to do . . .'

Nothing to do with what? With the murder? With his telephone calls? They were each speaking their own language, each pursuing their own idea, and they were all surprised that they couldn't understand one another.

7.

Lecoeur's gaze lighted on the telephone sitting on the table and he appeared to hesitate. Then he noticed a little plate with a white button and eventually he pressed it.

'May I . . . ? I don't know where it rings, but as long as it rings somewhere . . . We'll see whether someone comes . . .'

He felt the need for a break and they waited in silence, avoiding looking at one another. Of the three men, it was perhaps Pélardeau who was the calmest, the most composed, or at least outwardly. It is true that, as far as he was concerned, the game was up and he had nothing more to lose.

After a while, they heard footsteps echoing on an iron staircase, and then walking along a corridor, and another, and at last a discreet tap at the door.

'Come in!'

A squeaky-clean young officer entered who, compared to the three middle-aged men, gave the impression of a life force.

Lecoeur, who was a mere outsider there, asked him:

'Are you free for a moment?'

'Of course, sir. We were playing cards . . .'

'Would you guard Monsieur Pélardeau during our absence?'

The officer had no idea what was going on and looked with amazement at the elegant man being foisted on him.

'Gladly, sir . . .'

A few minutes later, Lecoeur and Maigret were outside on the peristyle. A canopy at the top of the steps sheltered them from the heavy rain slanting down through the darkness.

'I was suffocating in there . . . I thought you could probably do with some fresh air too . . .'

The huge cloud from which the flashes of lightning were coming was directly overhead and the wind was dropping. The street was empty except for the occasional passing car driving slowly and spraying water everywhere.

The chief of the Clermont-Ferrand Police Judiciaire lit a cigarette and watched the rain bouncing off the concrete and making the foliage in the garden tremble.

'I know that I got horribly bogged down, chief . . . I should have handed over to you . . .'

'What could I have done differently . . . ? You gained his trust . . . He'd reached a point where it seemed pointless answering your questions . . . He chose to say nothing, whatever happened . . . He's a man at the end of his tether, who was no longer responding, who accepted . . .'

'I had the impression . . .'

'You gradually wormed a few answers out of him . . . He started to show an interest . . . Then something happened which I don't understand yet . . . Something you said struck me . . .'

'What?'

'I don't know . . . All I know is that something clicked . . . I was watching his face all the time . . . Suddenly I saw an expression of utter amazement . . . We need to carefully weigh up all the words that were spoken . . . He was convinced we knew more . . .'

'That we knew what?'

Maigret said nothing and puffed on his pipe.

'A fact that is obvious to him, but which has eluded us . . .'

'Maybe I should have recorded our interview . . .'

'He would have kept quiet . . .'

'You really don't want to take over the questioning, chief?'

'Not only would that be irregular and, later, his lawyer would be able to use it against us, but I wouldn't fare any better than you, perhaps less well . . .'

'I don't know where to start and, worst of all, guilty as he is, I feel sorry for him . . . He's not the sort of criminal we generally have to deal with . . . When we left the hotel, earlier, I had the sense that a whole world had just brutally closed its doors on him . . .'

'He felt it too . . .'

'Do you think so?'

'He wanted to retain a certain dignity at all costs and he would consider any pity as charity . . .'

'I wonder whether he'll crack eventually . . .'

'He'll talk . . .'

'Tonight?'

'Perhaps . . .'

'On what ground?'

Maigret opened his mouth to say something, closed it again and went back to smoking his pipe. Then he continued evasively:

'At some point, not too soon, you could mention Mesnil-le-Mont . . . By asking him, for example, if he's ever been there . . .'

He appeared not to attach a great deal of importance to the question.

'Do you think he has?'

'I couldn't say . . .'

'Why would he have gone there, and what is the connection with the events in Vichy?'

'A vague hunch . . .' Maigret said apologetically. 'When you're swept away by the current, you cling on to anything you can . . .'

The officer on guard duty was also young and, in his eyes, the two men chatting under the canopy were prestigious figures who had reached the top of the hierarchy.

'I'd gladly have downed a glass of beer . . .'

There was a bar on the corner of the street, but there was no question of diving out into the deluge. As for Maigret, the word beer brought a resigned smile to his lips. He had promised Rian. He was keeping his word.

'Shall we go back up?'

They found the officer leaning against the wall. He straightened up with alacrity and stood to attention while the prisoner looked from one to the other.

'Thank you, officer. You may go . . .'

Lecoeur sat down at his desk and rearranged the notepad, pencil and telephone.

'I gave you a few minutes to think, Monsieur Pélardeau . . . I don't want to pester you with questions designed to confuse you . . . For the time being, I'm trying to get an idea . . . It isn't easy to enter directly into a man's life without making mistakes . . .'

He was seeking the right note, like the musicians in

the orchestra pit before the curtain goes up, and the man looked at him attentively, but without any visible emotion.

'You'd been married for some time, I imagine, when you met Hélène Lange?'

'I was over forty . . . I was no longer a young man and I'd been married fourteen years . . .'

'Was it a love marriage?'

'That is a word which takes on a different meaning as one gets older . . .'

'It wasn't a marriage of convenience?'

'No . . . It was my choice . . . And, on that matter, I have no regrets, other than the heartache I'm going to cause my wife . . . We are very good friends . . . We always have been and I've found her extremely understanding . . .'

'Even on the subject of Hélène Lange?'

'I didn't tell her about it . . .'

'Why not?'

He looked from one to the other.

'That is a subject that's difficult for me to talk about . . . I'm not a ladies' man . . . I have worked very hard during my life, and for a long time I perhaps remained quite innocent . . .'

'A passion?'

'I don't know the right word . . . I discovered a person who was completely different from everyone I knew . . . Hélène attracted me and terrified me . . . I found her intensity captivating . . .'

'You became her lover?'

'After a very long time . . .'

'Did she make you wait?'

'No. It was me . . . She hadn't had any affairs before me . . . But all this is run-of-the-mill for you, isn't it? I loved her . . . I mean, I thought I loved her . . . She asked for nothing, was content with a tiny place in my life, with those weekly visits you mentioned . . .'

'There was no question of your divorcing?'

'Never! Besides, I still loved my wife, in a different way, and I would never have agreed to leave her . . .'

Poor man! He was certainly more comfortable in his offices, his factories, or chairing a board meeting.

'Did she leave you?'

'Yes . . .'

Lecoeur glanced at Maigret.

'Tell me, Monsieur Pélardeau, have you ever been to Mesnil-le-Mont?'

He turned crimson, hung his head and stammered:

'No . . .'

'You knew she was there?'

'Not at the time . . .'

'You'd already broken up when she went there?'

'She'd told me that she would never see me again . . .'

'Why?'

Once more, stupefaction, incomprehension. Once more, the look of a man completely at a loss.

'She didn't want our child to . . .'

It was Lecoeur's turn to look puzzled whereas Maigret, ensconced in his chair, relaxed, like a big, contented cat, and didn't bat an eyelid.

'What child are you talking about?'

'But . . . Hélène's . . . About my son . . .'

He couldn't help saying the word 'son' with pride.

'You're saying she had a child with you?'

'Philippe, yes . . .'

Lecoeur seethed.

'She managed to get you to believe that . . .'

But Pélardeau patiently nodded.

'She didn't get me to believe anything . . . I have the proof . . .'

'What proof?'

'The birth certificate . . .'

'Drawn up by the mayor of Mesnil-le-Mont?'

'Naturally . . .'

'It gives the mother's name as Hélène Lange?'

'Of course . . .'

'And you didn't go to see this child whom you take to be your son?'

'Whom I take to be my son . . . Who *is* my son . . . I didn't go to see him because I didn't know where Hélène was giving birth . . .'

'Why the mystery?'

'Because she didn't want her child later to find himself in a situation . . . How can I put it . . . A difficult situation . . .'

'You don't think that those qualms are old-fashioned?'

'For some people, perhaps . . . Hélène too, in that sense, was old-fashioned . . . She had strong views on . . .'

'Listen, Monsieur Pélardeau . . . I think I'm beginning to understand, but we'll have to put the question of views aside for the time being . . . I apologize for becoming brutal . . . The facts exist, and we can't do anything about them, neither you nor I . . .'

'I don't see what you're suggesting . . .'

A vague anxiety was becoming apparent beneath his external self-assurance.

'Do you know Francine Lange?'

'No . . .'

'You never met her in Paris?'

'Never. Nor anywhere else . . .'

'Were you unaware that Hélène had a sister?'

'No . . . She mentioned she had a younger sister . . . They were orphans . . . Hélène had to leave school in order to work so that her sister . . .'

Unable to contain himself, Lecoeur jumped up, remaining on his feet, and if the office had been bigger, he would have started pacing up and down furiously.

'Go on . . . Go on . . .'

He wiped his hand across his brow.

'. . . So that her sister could receive the education that she deserved . . .'

'That she deserved, eh! . . . Don't hold it against me, Monsieur Pélardeau . . . I'm going to hurt you a great deal . . . I ought perhaps to go about it differently, prepare you for the truth . . .'

'What truth?'

'Her sister, at fifteen, worked in a hair salon in La Rochelle and was the mistress of a taxi-driver, before having I don't know how many lovers . . .'

'I read her letters . . .'

'Whose?'

'Francine's . . . She was at a famous Swiss boarding school . . .'

'Did you go there?'

'No, of course not . . .'

'Did you keep those letters?'

'I only skimmed them . . .'

'And, during that time, Francine was a manicurist in a luxury hotel on the Champs-Élysées . . . Are you beginning to understand? . . . Everything that you saw was a fabrication . . .'

The man was struggling. But his features, still set, were beginning to slacken and his mouth suddenly made such a pathetic grimace that Maigret and Lecoeur looked away.

'It isn't possible . . .' he stuttered.

'Sadly, it's the truth . . .'

'But why?'

It was a last appeal to destiny. For them to tell him straight away that it wasn't true, for them to admit that the police were making up these disgusting stories in order to fluster him . . .

'Forgive me, Monsieur Pélardeau . . . Until this evening, until these last few minutes, I too was unaware of the extent to which the two sisters had colluded . . .'

He was loath to sit down. He was still too on edge to do so.

'Hélène never spoke to you of marriage?'

'No . . .'

The 'no' was already less vehement.

'Even when she told you she was pregnant?'

'She didn't want to destroy my household . . .'

'So she did tell you . . .'

'Not in the way you mean . . . She told me she was going to disappear . . .'

'Kill herself?'

'There was no question of that . . . Because the child couldn't claim legitimacy . . .'

Lecoeur sighed and glanced at Maigret again. They understood each other. They imagined the scenes that must have taken place between Hélène Lange and her lover.

'You don't believe me . . . I myself . . .'

'Try and face up to the truth . . . It can only do you good . . .'

'Me, at the point where I am?'

He indicated the walls around him as if they were the walls of a prison.

'Let me finish, absurd as it may sound to you . . . She wanted to devote the rest of her life to bringing up our child the way she'd brought up her sister . . .'

'Without you ever seeing him?'

'How would she have explained my presence?'

'You could have been an uncle, a friend . . .'

'Hélène hated lies . . .'

Suddenly there was a note of irony in his voice, which was an encouraging sign.

'So she refused to allow your son to find out one day that you were his father?'

'Later, when he reached adulthood, she would have told him . . .'

He added in his wheezing voice:

'He's fifteen now . . .'

Lecoeur and Maigret maintained a painful silence.

'When I ran into her, in Vichy, I decided to . . .'

'Go on . . .'

'To see him . . . To find out where he was . . .'

'Did you find out?'

He shook his head and finally there were real tears in his eyes.

'No . . .'

'Where did Hélène tell you she was going to give birth?'

'In a village she knew . . . She didn't give the name . . . It was only two months later she sent me the birth certificate . . . The letter was postmarked Marseille . . .'

'How much money did you give her when she left?'

'Does it matter?'

'Very much . . . You'll see.'

'Twenty thousand francs . . . I sent her thirty thousand in Marseille . . . Then I insisted on giving her an allowance, so that our son could receive the best possible education . . .'

'Five thousand francs a month?'

'Yes . . .'

'What reason did she give for asking you to send the money to different poste-restante addresses?'

'She wasn't convinced of my strength of character . . .'

'Is that the expression she used?'

'Yes . . . In the end I agreed not to see the child until he was twenty-one . . .'

Lecoeur seemed to be asking Maigret:

'What do we do?'

And Maigret blinked two or three times, clenching the stem of his pipe harder between his teeth.

8.

Lecoeur had sat down again, slowly. He turned to the man with the devastated expression whom he'd just made suffer so many emotions and said, as if regretfully:

'I'm afraid I have more painful news for you, Monsieur Pélardeau . . .'

A bitter smile seemed to be saying: 'Do you think you can hurt me any more?'

'I have a lot of sympathy and even respect for the man you are . . . I am not playing games to extract the confession which in fact we don't need . . . What I have to tell you, like everything I have told you so far, is the strict truth, and I am sorry that it is so brutal . . .'

A pause, to give Pélardeau time to steel himself.

'You have never seen Hélène Lange's son . . .'

He expected a fierce objection, even a violent scene. But he found himself facing a defeated soul, who did not react or utter a word.

'You never suspected anything?'

Pélardeau looked up, shook his head and pointed to his throat to indicate that he couldn't speak straight away. He barely had the time to take his handkerchief out of his pocket before he was racked by an asthma attack even more violent than the last.

In the silence, Maigret became aware that outside too

silence had fallen, that the thunder had stopped and the rain was no longer bouncing off the paving stones.

'Forgive me . . .'

'It did occur to you to suspect the truth, didn't it?'

'Once . . . Only once . . .'

'When?'

'Here . . . The night when . . .'

'How many days before had you met her?'

'Two days . . .'

'Did you follow her?'

'From a distance . . . To find out where she lived . . . I was expecting to see her with my son, or to see him coming out of the house . . .'

'On Monday night, you appeared when she was about to go inside the house?'

'No . . . I saw the lodgers go out . . . I knew she'd be in the park, listening to the music . . . She's always loved music . . . I had no difficulty opening the door . . . My hotel room key worked . . .'

'You searched through the drawers.'

'First of all, I saw there was only one bed . . .'

'The photos?'

'Of her . . . Only her . . . I'd have given everything to come across a photo of a child . . .'

'And to discover letters?'

'Yes . . . I found myself facing an inexplicable void . . . Even if Philippe was at boarding school, he must . . .'

'She caught you in her house when she returned home?'

'Yes . . . I begged her to tell me where our son was . . .

I remember asking her if he'd died, if he'd had an accident . . .'

'She refused to answer?'

'She was calmer than I was . . . She reminded me of our pact . . .'

'The promise to give you back your son when he was twenty-one?'

'Yes . . . For my part, I'd sworn not to try and contact him . . .'

'Did she use to tell you about him?'

'In great detail . . . His first teeth . . . His childhood illnesses . . . The nanny she'd hired at a time when she was unwell . . . Then school . . . She gave me an almost day-by-day account . . .'

'Without mentioning the place?'

'Yes . . . Recently, he'd been saying he wanted to become a doctor, apparently . . .'

He looked at Lecoeur without false modesty.

'There never was any son?'

'There was . . . but he wasn't yours . . .'

'Another man?'

Lecoeur shook his head.

'It was Francine Lange who gave birth to a son, in Mesnil-le-Mont . . . Until you told me, I didn't know, I confess, that the child had been registered as being the son of Hélène Lange . . . The idea must have occurred to the two sisters when Francine found herself pregnant . . . If I know her, her first thought must have been to get rid of the baby . . . But her sister had a better idea . . .'

'That flashed through my mind . . . I told you . . . That

night, after begging her, I threatened . . . For fifteen years I've dreamed about this son whom I'd get to meet one day . . . My wife and I don't have any children . . . When I learned I was a father . . . But what's the use?'

'You put your hands round her neck?'

'To frighten her, to make her talk . . . I shouted at her to tell the truth . . . I didn't think of the sister, but I was afraid the child was dead, or disabled . . .'

He let his hands dangle as if there wasn't an ounce of energy left in his body.

'I squeezed hard . . . I didn't realize . . . If only her face had shown some kind of emotion! But no! She wasn't even afraid . . .'

'When you read in the newspaper that her sister was in Vichy, it gave you fresh hope?'

'If the child was alive, and if Hélène was the only person who knew where he was, there was no longer anyone to take care of him . . . I was expecting to be arrested from one day to the next . . . You must have found my fingerprints . . .'

'Without being able to compare them to yours . . . Even so, we'd have tracked you down eventually . . .'

'I had to know, to make arrangements . . .'

'You telephoned different hotels, in alphabetical order . . .'

'How do you know?'

It was child's play, but Lecoeur needed satisfaction.

'You called from different public phone booths . . .'

'So you'd identified me?'

'Almost . . .'

'What about Philippe?'

'Francine Lange's son was fostered shortly after his birth, by a family called Berteaux, farmers in Saint-André-du-Lavion, in the Vosges . . . With your money, the two sisters bought a hair salon in La Rochelle . . . Neither of them took care of the child, who continued to live in the country until, at two and a half, he fell into a pond . . .'

'He's dead?'

'Yes . . . But for you, he had to be kept alive, and Hélène invented his childhood, his first years at school, his games and, recently, his interest in medicine . . .'

'It's unspeakable . . .'

'Yes . . .'

'That a woman could . . .'

He shook his head.

'I am not doubting what you say . . . But something inside me refuses to accept this truth . . .'

'This is not the time occurrence of a case of this kind in the annals of crime . . . I could cite precedents . . .'

'No . . .' he begged.

He withdrew into himself, his resilience gone, with nothing left to cling to.

'You were right, earlier, when you said you didn't need a lawyer . . . All you need to do is tell your story to the jury . . .'

He remained completely still, his head in his hands.

'Your wife must be worried . . . In my opinion, the truth will hurt her less than what she might imagine . . .'

He appeared not to have thought about her and he finally showed his flushed face.

'What am I going to tell her?'

'I'm afraid you can't tell her anything at present . . . I'm not authorized to release you, even for a short time . . . I have to take you to Clermont-Ferrand . . . Unless the examining magistrate objects, which would surprise me, your wife will be allowed to visit you.'

This thought upset Pélardeau, who eventually looked at Maigret in desperation.

'Couldn't you talk to her?'

Maigret shot a questioning glance at Lecoeur, who shrugged as if to say that it wasn't up to him.

'I'll do my best . . .'

'You should tread softly, because for the past few years she's been suffering from a weak heart . . . Neither of us is young any more . . .'

Nor was Maigret. He felt old, this evening. He was impatient to get back to his wife, the humdrum daily walks through Vichy and the little yellow chairs in the park.

They went downstairs together.

'Shall I drop you off, chief?'

'I'd rather walk . . .'

The pavements were glistening. The black car drove off, taking Lecoeur and Pélardeau to Clermont-Ferrand.

Maigret lit his pipe and mechanically thrust his hands in his pockets. The night wasn't cold, but because of the storm the thermometer had still dropped by several degrees.

Water was dripping from the two shrubs flanking the entrance to the Hôtel de la Bérézina.

'It's you, at last!' sighed Madame Maigret, getting out

of bed to greet him. 'I dreamed you were at Quai des Orfèvres, carrying out an interrogation that went on for ever and having endless glasses of beer brought up . . .'

After watching him for a moment, she murmured:

'Is it over?'

'Yes . . .'

'Who is it?'

'A very respectable man, who employs thousands of office staff and workers, but who remained very unworldly . . .'

'I hope you'll be able to sleep tomorrow?'

'I'm afraid not . . . I have to go and explain to his wife . . .'

'She doesn't know?'

'No.'

'Is she here?'

'At the Hôtel des Ambassadeurs . . .'

'What about him?'

'In half an hour, he'll be inside Clermont-Ferrand prison . . .'

While he got undressed, she carried on watching him, finding there was something strange about him.

'How many years do you think he'll . . . ?'

And Maigret, filling his last pipe of the day, from which he only took a few puffs before getting into bed, said:

'I hope he'll be acquitted . . .'

OTHER TITLES IN THE SERIES

MAIGRET HESITATES
GEORGES SIMENON

'Maigret looked at him in some confusion, wondering if he was dealing with a skilful actor or, on the contrary, with a sickly little man who found consolation in a subtle sense of humour.'

A series of anonymous letters lead Maigret into the wealthy household of an eminent lawyer and a curious game of cat and mouse with Paris high society.

Translated by Howard Curtis

OTHER TITLES IN THE SERIES

MAIGRET'S PICKPOCKET
GEORGES SIMENON

'Maigret would have found it difficult to formulate an opinion of him. Intelligent, yes, certainly, and highly so, as far as one could tell from what lay beneath some of his utterances. Yet alongside that, there was a naïve, rather childish side to him.'

Maigret is savouring a beautiful spring morning in Paris when an aspiring film-maker draws his attention to a much less inspiring scene, one where ever changing loyalties can have tragic consequences.

Translated by Sian Reynolds

OTHER TITLES IN THE SERIES

MAIGRET AND THE NAHOUR CASE
GEORGES SIMENON

'*Maigret had often been called on to deal with individuals of this sort, who were equally at home in London, New York and Rome, who took planes the way other people took the Metro, who stayed in grand hotels . . . he had trouble suppressing feelings of irritation that might have been taken for jealousy.*'

A professional gambler has been shot dead in his elegant Parisian home, and his enigmatic wife seems the most likely culprit – but Inspector Maigret suspects this notorious case is far more complicated than it appears.

Translated by Will Hobson

OTHER TITLES IN THE SERIES

MAIGRET'S PATIENCE
GEORGES SIMENON

'Maigret felt less light at heart than when he had woken up that morning with sunlight streaming into his apartment or when he had stood on the bus platform, soaking up images of Paris coloured like in a children's album. People were often very keen to ask him about his methods. Some even thought they could analyse them, and he would look at them with mocking curiosity.'

When a gangster Maigret has been investigating for years is found dead in his apartment, the Inspector continues to bide his time and explore every angle until he finally reaches the truth.

Translated by David Watson

OTHER TITLES IN THE SERIES

MAIGRET DEFENDS HIMSELF
GEORGES SIMENON

'Maigret's cheeks turned red, as they had at school whenever he was called to the headmaster's office. 28 June ... He had been in the Police Judiciaire for more than thirty years, and the head of the Crime Squad for ten years, but this was the first time he had been summoned like this.'

When Maigret is shocked to find himself accused of a crime, he must fight to prove his innocence and save his reputation.

Translated by Howard Curtis

OTHER TITLES IN THE SERIES